SARAH'S WISH

SARAH'S WISH

a novel

Jim Baumgardner

TATE PUBLISHING & *Enterprises*

TATE PUBLISHING
& Enterprises

Sarah's Wish
Copyright © 2006 by Jim Baumgardner. All rights reserved.

Scripture quotations marked "KJV" are taken from the *Holy Bible, King James Version*, Cambridge, 1769. Used by permission. All rights reserved.

This novel is a work of fiction. However, several names, descriptions, entities and incidents included in the story are based on the lives of real people.

Published in the United States of America

ISBN: 1-5988690-9-4
06.12.22

To my grandchildren, whom I dearly love!
Caleb, Kyle, Timothy, Elizabeth, Chloe, Sarah, Corban and
Autumn, may this book bless your life, and give you an understanding
of the distance we have come and the journey yet to be completed.
– Papa

ACKNOWLEDGEMENTS

Writing any work about a subject which a person has not experienced can be difficult. I do not pretend to know or understand fully the hardships endured by slaves nor feelings produced from those trials. To gain a better appreciation of those dark days in American history I have spent many hours reading Ancestry.com's "Slave Narratives", owned by MyFamily.com, Inc., 2000. These documents contain interviews of former slaves describing their lives in bondage. I have tried to communicate some of their trials and feelings into Sarah's story. The "Slave Narratives" certainly enriched my understanding of a people doomed to a life of chains yet ever hoping for freedom. Anyone wishing a better understanding of slaves and slavery would be well served by reading these interviews.

Secondly, a book published in 1929, entitled *Thrills of the Historic Ohio River* by Frank Y. Grayson, was my resource for information about riverboats. Originally it was written as a series of daily river columns in the *Cincinnati Times-Star*. My copy of the book was edited by Barbara Fluegeman and published in 2000 by Spancil Hill Publishing Co. in Florence, Indiana.

SPECIAL NOTE

A portion of the proceeds from this book will go to the Maude Carpenter Children's Home in Wichita, Kansas. The Maude Carpenter home has been helping orphans like Sarah and children with special needs for over sixty years. May the Lord continue to bless the fine work being done at Maude Carpenter's.

Contents

Note to my readers

Please read the following words and phrases before you read the story. Included are nineteenth century terms that will help you understand your reading. As always, if you find another word you do not understand, look it up in a dictionary. I hope you like Sarah and enjoy her story.

Glossary of Terms

"A righteous man regardeth the life of his beast."
Proverbs 12:10 (KJV)

Apothecary: A nineteenth century drugstore where medicines were compounded and dispensed. It refers to the druggist, also. Apothecaries sold other items in addition to the medicines, much like today's drugstores.

Campbell, Alexander (1788–1866): preacher, president of Bethany College, Bethany, Virginia (later West Virginia), born: Scotland, died: Bethany, West Virginia, buried: family cemetery at Bethany

Cut shines: trying to trick someone

Fice dogs: worthless or mongrel dogs

Half-breed: People who had one Indian parent and one Caucasian parent were called half-breeds. As with other crude slang, the uneducated and bigoted used it. Running Fox's father was Shawnee and his mother, English. His mother schooled him, which accounts for his good English.

Hatchel: a tool for combing wool or separating flax fibers.

High-falutin': a person stuck on himself or herself, stuck up

Light a shuck: leave in a great hurry

Little end of the horn: getting or having less than expected

Moses: Refers to Harriett Tubman. A slave, she escaped from Maryland to Canada in 1849 but returned to Maryland several times to lead others to freedom. For our story, her title is used symbolically of all the heroes, black and white, that entered the South and led slaves to freedom on the Underground Railroad.

Mudsills: uneducated, lower class, common people

Orphan Train: The first Orphan Train left New York City, September 1854. The children taken west from 1854 to 1930 ranged from true orphans to many that were turned out into the streets of New York because their parents could no longer afford them.

Seven by nine: someone who is common or inferior

Slantindicular: slanting

Underground Railroad: A network of people in the northern states who helped slaves (before the Civil War) escape to freedom in Canada. One route ran from Cincinnati to Newport, (now Fountain City) Indiana, continuing northeast through Greenville, Ohio, and on to either Sandusky or Toledo, Ohio. There were also people in the South who helped runaways with their flight to freedom.

Wapakoneta: This Indian village became a town on March 2, 1849. German settlers helped the town grow into a successful city. Dr. John W. Baumgardner was one of those Germans. He served as Justice of the Peace in 1865.

Introduction

Many years ago families sat in their living rooms in the evening and listened to radio programs. With radio, imagination played a wonderful part. People did not see the action as they do now with television. Hearing a squeaking door caused a person to imagine all kinds of reasons for the squeak. The eagerness of knowing what would happen next kept the listener on the "edge of their seat."

As you read this book I want you to imagine yourself as a bystander in each scene. You are there, and the story unfolds now, not in the distance past. Imagine listening to that radio, and in your "mind's eye" you see, and hear, and taste, and smell, and touch nineteenth century Ohio.

The story begins one stifling hot afternoon. Do you feel the heat? Taste the dust? Smell the horseflesh? Hear the laughter of mother and daughter? And – see that snake! You are in 1858.

Hang on – *here we go!*

I

The Accident

It all seemed to have happened in one of those slow-motion moments. Actually, the horse heard it first – the rattle sound. The sound that leaves goose bumps on a big man's neck. By the time the girl caught eye of it, Blackie had instinctively shied to the right.

"Snake!" Rachel pointed at the coiled serpent, its mouth gaping, fangs laid bare.

Blackie bolted. The sudden jerk slammed Rachel against the seat, wrenching the reins from her hands. Immediately she reached for twelve-year-old Sarah. Careening wildly along the narrow lane they furiously clutched at the buggy seat.

"Blackie!" Rachel screamed. "Whoa! Whoa, Blackie!"

The frightened horse raced on at full gallop while the reins dragged the ground. Mother and daughter tightened their grip and waited for Blackie to run himself out.

"Blackie!" Sarah screamed. "Stop, Blackie! Oh, please! Stop! Mama, I'm scared!"

Rachel shrieked louder, "Whoa!"

The lane curved sharply right, but the frantic horse dashed straight on. Ten feet into a meadow the buggy struck the outcroppings of a stump and shot Rachel down the seat smashing into Sarah. Flipping onto its side the buggy slammed the ground, digging in. Dirt and grass flew in all directions. Breaking loose from the splintered buggy, Blackie made a blue streak through the wild flowers and disappeared into the woods.

The dust settled – silence.

Cracking her eyelids, Sarah peeked through the narrow slits, dimly aware of the pain. It burned. Yes, it felt like fire shooting through every inch of her body. A dream – sure that was it. She dreamed a restless dream. Darkness surrounded her, and she hated the dark. Her breathing tightened, her chest ached, and the darkness squeezed her whole body without mercy. She hated tight spaces, and she despised snakes. Both were unbearable, and both were crammed into the grayness from which she could not awake. The girl lay crumpled in the short grass for several minutes. Finally, the burning streaked up her arm, jolting her awake. Not a dream, she quickly realized the arm was broken, and the pain would not go away anytime soon.

"Mama!" she screamed. "Mama!" Her face flushed prickly hot. Pushing to a sitting position she bawled loudly, "Mama! Mama! Where are you?"

Her darting eyes searched the wreckage for any sign of movement. Finally, she struggled to her feet, clutched her arm, and wobbled toward the smashed buggy.

Almost stumbling over her mother, she hesitated, not wanting to believe it. "Oh, Mama," the girl groaned. Seeing broken wood and metal pinning Rachel against the ground, she fought hard to gather her wits.

Her face tightened with pain as she stared at the rubble. Then, pushing with all her might, Sarah tried to move it with her good arm. It wouldn't budge, and her heart sank. Dropping to her knees, the girl gently brushed dirt from her mother's face.

"Wake up, Mama."

Calm settled on the meadow. Birds chirped to each other, but the sound for which Sarah's heart begged did not come. Her mother remained quiet.

"Please, wake up."

She held the limp hand. Unable to speak the words, Sarah thought them. *Oh, Mama, you're dying.* She touched her mother's face, no response.

"Mama, I must go for help." Her lips trembled. "I don't want to leave you, but you need the doctor."

A hush spread over the meadow, even the birds stopped talking.

"Oh, what should I do? I wish you could tell me. Wake up and tell me!"

A small, white-winged butterfly landed softly on a wildflower next to Rachel.

Sarah leaned over and kissed her mother's soft hand. "What will happen to Joseph and Polly? They need you, Mama. Tonight – what about tonight? I promised never to tell. What should I do now?" she begged, her tone frantic. "Tell me! Please wake up, Mama. Oh, Please! I need you. Oh, Mama, don't leave me."

Blinded by tears the girl buried her face against her mother's shoulder. Silently fluttering its wings, the pretty butterfly skipped over to Rachel's bruised cheek. The quiet settled in, like silence at twilight in a well-kept cemetery.

Sarah began to pray.

Suddenly, Rachel's eyes opened and a pretty smile skipped across her lips. She saw them and was not afraid. The angels had come. Slowly her eyelids fluttered shut, and the butterfly quietly winged its way into the blue.

2

Strangers

"That's her," the man said, pointing, "the one with the dark curly hair – standing by the old lady."

"Looks like her ma," the old gray-bearded man spat the words, sneering. "Too bad about her ma and that accident," he mocked through a crooked smile.

Folks from around the county had begun to arrive at the little cemetery on the edge of town. Doctor Baumgardner stood near the coffin, nodding a friendly greeting as young and old alike surrounded the grave. The town folks had shortened Doc's name to Baum, and he had accepted it. He had become a friend to almost everyone in the county, and they counted on him when sick and hurting. Sarah stood next to Doctor Baum with Mary Martin on the girl's left side. Granny Evans, another good friend of Rachel's, took a position right behind Sarah.

As they waited for the service to begin, each one thought about Rachel. Doc wondered if he could have saved her if he had been there. Mary thought about the letter Rachel had given her the year before. It was to be opened if she were to die. Mary read it that morning before coming to the cemetery. Rachel wrote that Sarah knew a secret and promised to never tell, but the letter did not share the secret with Mary. The woman thought it strange that Rachel would not reveal the secret to her best friend.

Just outside the cemetery fence, a slight distance away, Sarah noticed two strangers sitting astride their horses, each wearing a gun belt. A shock of gray hair hung below the hat of the old fellow, and a gray beard that ended in a point covered his face. He leaned forward and rested on the saddle horn, keeping his shadowy eyes on her. The other man had a sharp hatchet face, with thick eyebrows. He sat quite tall in the saddle – arrow straight. His eyes, dark as coal, moved slowly back and forth. Something interested him, something that kept his eyes glued to the countryside.

"Rachel Smith, born June 15, 1822, awoke to life immortal on June 3, 1858." Thus, the old preacher, Brother Franklin, began his remarks at the gravesite.

"The Lord giveth and the Lord taketh away, blessed be the name of the Lord."

Closing the Bible, he slowly scanned the crowd.

"Only moments ago Rachel's good friend, Mary Martin, told me of a letter written last year. It was from Rachel. In it she said she had no fear of dying, because she trusted in her Lord. She requested that in the event of her death Sarah was to be placed in a good home and given Christian teaching. We know Mary, Rachel's trustworthy friend, along with the good doctor, will fulfill her wish."

A nodding of heads and a small number of "amens" came from all corners.

"He be right about that," Granny Evans whispered in Sarah's ear. The girl nodded in agreement.

The preacher paused, and the crowd waited in silence. Sarah lifted her eyes and caught a quick peek at the strangers. The old man continued to stare, and it raised goose bumps on her arms.

The preacher, dressed in his black broadcloth suit, took a breath, once more surveyed the congregation, and then began his sermon.

Several minutes later the girl muttered quietly to herself. "Why Mama?" She lowered her head choking on her tears. "Why did God take you? They need you – I need you!"

Everyone looked Sarah's way, unable to make out her words of misery. The two strangers still sat astride their mounts, and from under the brim of his grimy hat, Graybeard persisted with his icy stare. It seemed to come from a face of stone.

"God will provide." Brother Franklin looked over at the girl. "He will care for you."

A smile crossed the old gentleman's face, so big his face seemed to light up the day. Stepping forward he placed his hand on the coffin and continued on with kind words.

Sarah again looked to see what the men were doing. The tall man never took his eyes from the countryside, ignoring the funeral completely.

They're not here to remember Mama. Suddenly, a shiver went through her, and she understood who they were and why they had come.

"This good woman," the preacher tapped the coffin, "did many fine deeds. Her wonderful work went far beyond what anyone knows, except those she helped and the good Lord Himself.

"Sarah," his eyes were serious, "you'll make it fine in this life because you had a wonderful mother."

"Mama, I'll help," she muttered. "I'll take care of them."

Granny Evans patted her shoulder, understanding her words quite well. She also knew she would be the one who must care for the girl. Nothing got by Granny, and sure not this girl's problems. She had been to the farm many times, keeping up with Rachel and her work. She knew the secret, and also knew Sarah would keep it.

What's Sarah talking about? The doctor spoke to himself. *Take care of what? Is it her animals?*

Placing his Bible on top of Rachel's coffin and bowing his head, Brother Franklin offered a prayer for the woman and her daughter.

The words and conduct of the old minister brought a bit of comfort to Sarah. The preacher had a good reputation in town, and he regularly passed through Auglaize County. The old fellow had been in a nearby town when news came of Rachel's death. As a close friend of the family he started immediately for Wapakoneta.

The old man continued in prayer, but Sarah found it difficult to listen. Her mind wandered. She thought herself homeless, and of course she was now an orphan. *Oh, Mama, I'm so lonely. I don't think I can stand it. Only two days ago you were here, now I'm alone. What am I going to do? What?*

Glancing to her right, she glared at the two strangers. They chose to insult Mama by refusing to remove their hats.

"May the Lord bless you and keep you and make his face shine upon you. Through our Lord we pray, Amen."

Finishing his remarks the old man hastily moved to Sarah's side. Stooping down, he hugged her, and turning to Mary he did the same.

Doc stood watching as Brother Franklin spoke in a low voice to the girl. He wondered about her coming days. Where would she go? *She's only twelve years old and will live with a family for quite awhile. Mary really isn't able to take on any more. She already has a large brood of chickabiddies.* Doc quietly chuckled at the thought, although it did not seem right at a funeral. The pressing need of a home for Sarah kept the doctor flustered. *For now she's staying with Mary, but it's temporary, a few days at most.*

Needing to make his rounds, he put the problem aside for the moment and hurried over.

"I'm sorry about your mother, Sarah. We will help you through this terrible time."

Hugging her, he told her not to worry about a place to live. The townspeople loved her, and she would not be homeless. Sarah nodded her head, eyes downcast.

All of a sudden, she grabbed his coat sleeve. "Doctor, I need to go home! May I borrow your horse?"

A strange request at her mother's funeral, Doc thought. "Sarah, I have calls to make, maybe Mary will take you tomorrow. Do you need to get your clothes?"

"Yes! I want my clothes, right now." Her tone sounded more demanding than a simple request.

"I'm sure Mary will let you wear one of her daughter's dresses until you get your own."

"That's right, Sarah. Martha doesn't mind sharing her clothes. You're wearing one of her dresses now, don't you remember?"

"No, I must go today. I can't wait!"

Mary was puzzled by Sarah's uncharacteristic behavior.

"I don't want you to go with me. I can go alone. I want to go alone!

I know my way, and it's not far. Mrs. Martin let me use your horse, please!" Her face twisted into a frown. "I'll return before dark."

Mary looked her over and again peeked at the doctor. "Sarah, I can't let you go by yourself. I'll take you in the carryall tomorrow morning."

"Mrs. Martin, I must go today, and by myself."

"Sarah," Doc stared straight into the girl's eyes. "What's so important that you must go right now?"

"Uh, well, uh, I have to take care of Blackie," the words slipped out.

"Sarah, you know Blackie is at the livery," Doc told her straight, but in a gentle voice.

"I know, but we have other animals. Let's see – ten chickens and a cow and . . ."

"Sarah, I sent Jake over there this morning to check on them. Everything is fine. The troughs have plenty of water and feed, and the cow is in the pasture."

"You sent Jake," her voice trembled the words, "Did he say anything when he returned?"

What strange behavior! "Jake fed and watered the animals and everything is fine today. I want you to rest and stop worrying. It's been a trying time since your mother passed."

Sarah broke into tears as once again Mary turned down her request. The carryall awaited, and she moped slowly toward it.

"Mary, I'll drop by after dinner to check on Sarah."

"Thank you, Doctor," she called over her shoulder.

Having several stops before noon, Doc hurried to his buggy. Giving a side-glance at Mary, he saw Sarah again pleading with her. Mary continued to shake her head, saying, "No, not today."

He scratched his beard, thinking it over. *Why does Sarah continue to pester her? There's something more to this than wanting to care for a few chickens or get her clothes. Yes, this is mighty strange indeed.*

As he picked up the reins, Doc saw one of the town's shopkeepers in conversation with the mounted strangers. *Hmmm, who are*

3

A Secret Place

Sarah knew Pistol was quite gentle, so it was easy to climb two rungs of the ladder, get on the sorghum barrel and mount the horse. As she walked Pistol toward her farm northeast of town, Sarah considered what she had done. Feeling guilty for sneaking out the window and taking the horse from the barn, she wondered about her punishment.

I must go home today – it can't wait! It's already been two days. I can return before they know I'm gone. If I don't, if I get caught, well – I won't tell them anything! Even if they whip me, I won't tell. I can't let Mama down. She knows when I'm doing good things, and God keeps the bad from her. She doesn't know I stole Mrs. Martin's horse. Besides, I'm only borrowing it for a few hours. I don't think they will hang me for horse thieving. No, I only borrowed it!

Crossing a little bridge over the narrow creek she rode another quarter mile. Instead of making straight for the hitching post in front of the house, she gently nudged Pistol toward the apple orchard. With the broken arm secure in the splint that Doctor Baum placed on it, she used the other one to hold the reins and steady herself. Although it was her forearm and not really a bad break, still it ached terribly. She tried to ignore it and pushed on.

Peering intently down each row of apple trees, she nudged Pistol along the fence that corralled the milk cow. Bessie looked up from her grazing, saw Sarah, and returned to dinner. At the chicken house she slid from the horse. Cautiously opening the door the girl peeked inside. Several chickens nesting on their eggs made clucking sounds. Finding nothing out of place, she headed north across the barnyard.

The latch moved easily, and the barn door opened after a light tug. She pulled the big door wide open, shooting a rectangle of light into the barn. The smell of hay filled her nose with its sweet fragrance as she stepped into the shadows. Slowly, her eyes adjusted to the dim light, and she found everything in place.

Sam and Eliza Smith planted the rye grass to cut for hay and other crops grown on the farm. At harvest time they shared the crop with Rachel. The Negroes' cabin stood a half-mile away on the other side of the woods. Many people did not want the Smiths on Rachel's property, but Sarah remembered her mother saying, "It is none of their business who I have on my land." Sarah knew color of skin really created the dislike for the Smiths. Free Negroes like Sam, Eliza, and their daughter, Esther, remained objects of hatred of many Northerners.

"The Smiths had been with her family ever since Sarah could remember. Her grandfather had freed all his slaves years before she was born. All the slaves had left, except the Smiths. They had continued to work for Grandfather, and he paid them fair wages. After Grandfather died, Sarah's daddy moved to western Ohio, and the Smiths came with him.

The former slaves helped build the special house and outbuildings. At age seven Sarah learned of the secret hiding place for runaway slaves. She promised to keep the secret and had always kept her word.

Quietly shutting the barn door and latching it, she dashed toward the little carriage barn that served as Blackie's home. It sat about twenty feet from the house. Hay that had been cut in the nearby meadow filled the width of the back wall and all the way up to the ceiling. Sarah opened the door and peeped inside. Pulling her head back, she again looked one way and the other. Inside she glanced at the small door on the sidewall. It remained shut. Gazing at the empty stall, her eyes brimmed with tears. She recalled seeing Blackie race through the meadow, and then came the dark.

"Hello," Sarah called softly. "Hello!"

Waiting several seconds and not hearing anything, she closed the door. Racing along a pathway lined with her mother's rose bushes, the girl arrived at the front of the house. When the bushes bloomed with beautiful petite yellow roses, this walkway became her favorite place.

Near the front steps she stooped and turned over a large rock. Sarah picked up a key and again took a glimpse of the property. Satisfied no one was watching, she stuck the key into the lock. Rapidly turning the glass doorknob, she opened the front door and darted inside. Pulling the key out, she quickly shut and locked the door. Slipping the key into her pocket, Sarah turned and stared at the bookcase on the far wall.

A wide staircase sat against the back wall, and the bookcase nestled into the alcove made by the stairs. A second much smaller bookcase had been placed into the alcove across the width of the stairs, making an "L" shaped area to hold Eli's books. The small, two shelved bookcase stood about three feet high. The large one had several shelves full of her daddy's books. Rachel never let them go and occasionally read from them. Sarah walked toward the small bookcase and stopped next to it. Sliding her hand across the top shelf as though dusting, she considered what to do.

Upstairs!

Bounding up the stairs to her bedroom door, she rushed in. Finding nothing out of place and touching nothing, she closed the door and entered her mother's bedroom. Nothing! She did the same in the other two upstairs bedrooms, again nothing. Rushing downstairs and into the kitchen, she spotted a bowl of apples Rachel had placed on the table. Sarah opened the cupboard and drew out a loaf of bread her mother had baked the morning of the accident. It wasn't fresh, but it would have to do. In a bag she placed the bread, all of the apples, a jar of apple butter, along with a spoon and a large butcher knife. Grabbing the bag, she sprinted to the bookcase.

Carefully, Sarah removed the books from the small bookcase and placed them on the floor. She moved a vase containing one wilting rose and sat it on a shelf of the larger bookcase. It only took one hand to easily slide the small bookcase. To keep from scratching the floor it had a piece of heavy cloth glued onto the bottom. Scratch marks must not be seen. Now, the girl opened the bag and removed the knife. The end fit tightly into a tiny crack in the wall. Sarah pushed gently sideways on the knife as she pulled back. The wall moved. A small door appeared, and she tugged with the ends of her fingers on the edge of the little door. It opened. Inside the wall, in the small area under the stairs, Sarah lifted a little handle recessed into a trap door. She jerked, and the door popped out of the floor.

"Hello! Hello there," she gave a loud whisper as she leaned into the darkness. "It's Sarah. Are you there?"

Silence.

"Joseph, Polly, I have food. Hello! Joseph, Polly." *Oh my, they're dead! What'll happen now? No – not possible, it's only been two days. No one starves to death in two days.*

Replacing the trap door she closed the wall. Taking the bag, Sarah entered the kitchen, replaced the knife into the cupboard drawer, and walked out the backdoor. Trudging slowly, and keeping an eagle eye on the lane, she reached the corner of the carriage barn. Seeing no one and thinking it safe to enter, the girl dashed inside.

Her broken arm ached, and the good one needed rest from carrying the sack. She dropped it with a clunk and leaned against the ladder leading to the hayloft. The girl did not have the strength to pull herself up the rungs. With one good arm, and needing to bring the sack along, too, it simply was not going to happen.

"Joseph, Polly," she mouthed, almost whispering.

Silence, except for a few flies buzzing about the horse stalls.

"Joseph, Polly."

Nothing except silence filled her ears. Her shoulders slumped. Grabbing the bag, Sarah dragged it behind as she tromped over and plopped on a mound of hay. It was the spot where Blackie rested at sleeping time.

What now? Where can they be? They need me, and I've let them down!

Tears sprung to her dark brown eyes. With her mother gone forever, and now this – it had become too much for the girl to handle. Rivers of tears streamed down her cheeks and dripped from her chin, wetting her borrowed dress.

4

Missing

"Mother, where's Sarah?" Jane, the Martin's oldest daughter, asked. "I thought she might take a walk with me."

"She's sleeping. I don't think Sarah is up to it," Mrs. Martin replied firmly. "She's worn out. Tell the children to come home and tend to their chores. It's almost suppertime."

"The bedroom window is open, so I looked in. She's gone!"

"What? She can't be gone. Oh, maybe she's down at the outhouse. Run out there, and make sure she's all right."

Jane scooted out the back door and down a narrow path. Knocking on the outhouse door she called out, "Sarah! Sarah, are you in there?"

"Yes, it's me. I'm in here," came a high-pitched voice.

"Jake, you stop right now. I'm telling Mother on you."

"No, Jane. It's really me – Sarah."

Again the fake high-pitched voice tried to fool her. It didn't work.

"That does it, Jake. I'm telling Mother right now, and she'll be madder than a wet hen! Sarah is missing, and we don't have time for your foolishness."

Jake shoved the door and jumped out. "What do you mean she's missing? Is someone looking for her?"

"Jake, you beat all. Don't you have a lick of sense?" Jane shook her head. "The doctor wants her to rest since she's had a rough week. Her mother died!"

"I know. Do you think I'm stupid?"

"Well, you act like it sometimes."

"So do you! Sometimes."

"Leave me alone, Jake. If you won't help at least get out of the way."

Jane brushed past him and jogged up the path toward the house. Bursting through the kitchen door she exclaimed, "Mother, Mother, Sarah's not there! She's missing. Maybe she ran away. Maybe she's visiting the cemetery. She talks to her mother all the time. I have a friend at school . . ."

"Jane! We don't have time. We have to find Sarah before dark."

Jake opened the kitchen door, and immediately Mary yelled for his help.

"I'll help," he left off the joking. "What do you want me to do?"

"Run to the pond and have your brothers and sisters hightail it home," she ordered. "We'll begin a search while you saddle Pistol and light out for Doctor Baum's place. Tell him he's needed."

"I'll get the others, but I can't ride for the doctor."

"You'll do both, Jake, and not another back talk word from you!"

"Mother, I think Sarah stole our horse."

"Jake, have you gone plum out of your mind?" Jane butted in. "Mother, tell him this is serious and to stop his silliness. Father needs to take a strap to him."

"Mind your own business, Jane." Jake glared at her. "You think you know everything. Well you don't. Now . . ."

"Jake, don't give me anymore silly talk. We are wasting time." Mary pushed him through the doorway. "Now get the other children."

"Mother, I'm going, but you should listen to me," the boy muttered. "Sarah rode out on a horse, and it looked like Pistol. I saw her when I was fishing. I got me a catfish. He weighed about . . ."

Mary jerked like she was bee stung. Snatching him by his shirt, she stammered, "Wait – hold on a moment, little man. Why didn't you tell me this earlier? Are you . . . are you saying she left hours ago?"

"Yes, ma'am. I saw her headin' north toward her place. Nobody asked me about it, so I thought nuttin of it. Now, I know she's a horse thief." Jake nodded his head, crossing his arms on his chest.

"Jake, she's not a horse thief. I don't want you saying that again." Mary shook her finger at him, and the boy got rid of the smirking face.

"You fetch yourself over to Mr. Brown's, borrow a horse and ride to town. Ask Doctor Baum to get here right away. Can you do it, boy?"

"Yes, ma'am, right now." He streaked through the back door and down the path that led to the neighbor's place.

"What am I going to do with that boy? Jane, make sure Pistol isn't in the barn, and then find your brothers and sisters. Send Martha to tell Harold and your father what's happened. We need them."

"I'm on my way, Mother."

"Look at that, Polly, it's Missy Saree. She looks done in. I thoughts I heared a little voice. Can't hear so well in that wall."

"I told you. I knowed I was a hearin' a little voice. I wonder where Miss Rachel is. I thought they done up and left us."

"Missy Saree, Missy Saree." Joseph bent down and touched her arm. "Polly, she done gotten herself hurt." He pointed at the splint.

"Land-a-Goshen, she is. Sarah!"

The girl squinted, looking up into the black face of Joseph.

"Huh!"

"Missy Saree, what you doin' here? Where you all been?" The man had a polite manner about him, but the voice sounded urgent. "Where Miss Rachel?"

Sarah's dark eyes attempted to focus on the man, all the while trying to clear her head. Finally realizing what had happened, the girl struggled to sit up.

"Oh my, I fell asleep. I have to go!" she shrieked. "They'll come here! I have to go now!"

Still clutching the bag, she got to her feet. She thrust the small supply of food at Joseph.

"It's all I have today. I'm sorry. I'll come tomorrow," she gasped. "I have to go before they get here."

The girl raced to open the door.

"Oh no!" She whirled about. "I forgot. Ham and other things are in the cellar. I'll get them tomorrow. Please don't go outside. It's too dangerous. Now, boost me onto my horse. Please hurry!"

Joseph lifted her, and she climbed onto Pistol's back.

"Sarah, where's Miss Rachel?" Polly's lips trembled the words as she wrung her hands in worry. "We must talk to her. Where's we to go?"

"I'll tell you tomorrow. Please, stay inside. Tomorrow is the day. I must go!"

Digging her heels into Pistol's sides, the pony gave a slight jerk and trotted away. Polly turned her eyes to Joseph. The man raised his arms, and she wearily fell into his embrace.

"Oh Joseph, I is so afraid!"

Tenderly he patted her back. "I know, Polly. I shore nuff is, too."

Riding along the lane and turning onto the road Sarah headed south toward town. Quickly she pulled rein and considered what to do. Finally, she brought the horse about.

I have to go back. Polly and Joseph's lives may depend on it.

Her arm ached. She ignored it and crossed the little bridge. Arriving at the hitching post Sarah slid off Pistol and climbed the steps. Dashing to the bookcase, she shoved it in front of the secret door. After replacing the books and vase, she darted to the back door. Setting the lock, Sarah backtracked, rushing to the front porch. After locking the door, the girl raced down the steps and put the key under the rock.

"Whew," she sighed aloud. "Now, how am I gonna get up there, Pistol?"

Looking for something to boost her, she decided to lead him alongside the porch. Mounting the steps the girl climbed onto the railing, then plunk. Sarah landed on the horse.

Hoof beats! Someone's coming! She turned sharply to see a carriage crossing the bridge. *Mrs. Martin's carriage! Put on your thinking cap Sarah, you've been seen. They cannot know. They must not know! Mama always kept the secret. Now it's my secret. I promised!*

31

As the carriage neared the house, she saw Mary and the doctor.
Oh, my! What to do?

"Whoa," Doc barked, reining the horse to a stop.

All three eyed each other. An uncomfortable silence followed, and Sarah didn't like it.

"Sarah," Mary called from the carriage. "Are you all right?"

Maybe I can sidetrack them. I don't want them to ask me questions I can't answer. "No, Mrs. Martin, my arm is hurting." She puckered her face into a pained look. "It's hard to ride with only one good hand." Then, with a pout that would melt the coldest heart, she stared directly into Doc's eyes. "I think I need medicine for the ache."

"Hmmmm, Doctor, do you have something?" Mary's tone revealed her uncertainty about the girl's answer.

Stepping from the carriage, he reached into his black bag. "Sarah, I have a pill. Do you have water inside?" He pointed at the door.

"No," she mumbled. Quickly raising her voice, "We can draw it from the well. Would you, please?"

"I sure will."

As she slowly drank, the girl thought of what to say next, but her eyes never moved off Mary. Finishing, she handed the tin cup back to Doc. "May I ride in the carriage?"

"You may. We have room for a young lady," she quipped. "Pistol can trot along behind. He knows the way home."

Thinking there would be no more questions, she breathed a sigh of relief. "I'm worn out." Sliding off the horse, she shuffled over.

"Where are your clothes?"

She wasn't supposed to ask any more questions. "My clothes?" she echoed with impish eyes.

"Yes, isn't that why you came here?" Mary searched her face for a clue to the girl's mysterious behavior.

"Well, uh, I wanted to see about Bessie and the chickens. I saw them all right, and they're fine." Sarah tried her best to avoid the clothes question. "Well, let's go."

"Sarah, let's get your clothes while we're here. You said you wanted them."

The girl stared hard at Mary. She didn't like the woman's persistence about the clothes. Then, her eyes darted, giving Doc a marble-eyed side-glance.

Now what? Mama told me to always tell the truth, but this is hard. I can't let anyone harm Joseph and Polly. They're more important. "Uh, I can't get them." She barely tiptoed on the edge of truth. "The house is locked. I can't get in without a key."

"The house is locked? We never lock our house. I don't know of any thieves around here." Mary gave the doctor a suspicious look. "Why would Rachel lock the house?"

"Mama and I live here alone. We don't have a man to protect us, and sometimes we're afraid. We always lock the house."

Choosing her words carefully so not to lie, she kept other reasons for the locked house to herself.

"Makes sense," Doc agreed, "it would be scary living here alone."

Sarah nodded her head in agreement, studying Mary's face for any hint of doubt.

"Rachel's things are at my house," Mary remembered. "Doctor, you gave them to me the other day, and I kept them for Sarah. Is there a key in those things?"

"I believe so."

"I'm sure of it." Sarah's big brown eyes sparkled. "Mama carried it in her little handbag."

Mary continued to press her. "Do you have a key?"

Fighting back tears, she answered, but it came without thinking.

"No," she squeaked. *Why does she keep pushing? I don't want trouble! I don't want to lie.*

The girl saw it in Mary's eyes. The doubt Sarah hoped would not be in there was.

Mrs. Martin suspects something!

Fretting, Sarah tried to think it through. She knew her answer had not been a lie, but it came too close, and she didn't like it.

The key under the rock is Mama's, not mine. But, is it mine now, since Mama is no longer here? "No, I don't have a key. Mama never gave me a key to carry."

Now, she tried to convince herself of what she took on as her answer. *It's true. So I'm not lying, but it's as close as I want to get. Please don't ask me anything else,* she pleaded silently. "I'll come tomorrow." With that she gave a mischievous grin. "I'm hungry!"

Mary gawked at Doc, and he returned the stare. Finally, the woman remembered the letter.

"Sarah has a secret and is keeping a promise." Rachel's words! Mary's mind screamed. *"Sarah has a secret and is keeping a promise."* Mary ran those words through her mind, over and over. *What's the secret? What's she hiding? What did Rachel mean? Oh, my dear, dear friend, why didn't you tell me all of it?*

At the same moment, the doctor had his own thoughts about the girl's actions. *I can't put my finger on it, but something isn't quite right here. Sarah's behavior is strange and her words betray her. She's keeping something inside, and the death of her mother is only part of it.*

Rubbing his beard, he faintly shook his head. He had to think on those things. Maybe an answer would come sooner or later.

"Let me help you, young lady." Climbing in after her, they headed for home.

5

Slave Catchers!

A loud rooster squawk forced open Sarah's eyelids. The first rays of dawn gently streamed through the window pane touching the far side of the bedroom. Peeping through blurry eyes, she became faintly aware of the flowery wallpaper and the soft tweet of the morning birds. Trying hard to clear the night's sleep from her head, she began to think about Polly and Joseph.

They were so frightened. I must do something, today! I need a plan.

The runaways tapped on Rachel's front door late Tuesday night. After feeding and settling them in, Rachel planned the delivery of her "packages" to the next station on Thursday night. She died Thursday afternoon.

I'll have to do it myself. Tonight, somehow, someway, I'll make the delivery. I've gone with Mama before. I've even gone by myself, the time Mama was too sick to go. Oh, I want to tell Mrs. Martin. Yet, Mama said tell no one.

Rachel knew that confiding in anyone invited more danger. Folks did not want to get involved. A tunnel running under the house ended at the carriage barn. Many escaping slaves hid in the secret place and moved on at night through the apple orchard toward the next station. They had a final destination of Sandusky or Toledo.

The slaves wanted freedom from their masters in the South, and certain brave souls took the risk of escaping across the Ohio River. Help for the runaways came from folks along the Underground Railroad, a railway that did not run on tracks. Kind folks like Moses helped Southern slaves move from one house, called a "station," further north to the next station. Those who helped called themselves "conductors" or "agents." The slaves made their way through the Northern states to Canada because there they could be completely free.

The Smith family had helped runaways for years. When Rachel told Sarah about the "packages," she insisted the girl keep the secret. Lives depended on not telling anyone. Numerous times "packages" arrived, and Sarah never knew. Rachel realized if questioned by the "slave catchers," Sarah would not have to lie. Her mother wanted to help the runaways, but she insisted they not lie. Sometimes it took all of her "wits" to avoid questions. Her mother could have been arrested for breaking the Fugitive Slave Law. Ohio state law held that people could not own slaves, but America's federal law required people in the Northern states to not help runaways from the slave states, either. Any captured runaway must be returned to his master in the South.

I'll sneak out of the house tonight and move my packages by myself. Mama wants me to do it. If the law arrests me, well, maybe they'll go easy on me since I'm a little girl, not too little though. I'm twelve, yet people think I'm younger 'cause I'm short. Good, they'll think I'm too young to go to jail. Still, if I have to . . . I'll go. I won't tell where the slaves came from or where they're going. The girl closed her eyes, continuing to mull it over in her mind.

"They can whip me, and I still won't tell," Sarah blurted aloud.

"What did you say?" asked Jane as she rubbed her eyes awake.

"Oh, nothing."

"Who's going to whip you? Mother isn't going to whip you because you went to your house yesterday, but don't do it again. She worried herself sick about you."

"I know she won't whip me, Jane."

Sarah said nothing further and kept quiet about going home by herself. She must, and she knew it. The runaways could not be left in the cellar room another night.

The old preacher finished his sermon and dismissed the congregation. Immediately he marched to where Sarah sat with the Martins.

"How's Sarah this fine Sunday?"

"I'm better, sir." Sarah raised her splint. "My arm isn't hurting as much as the first day."

"Good, good, I'm glad to hear it." His ruddy face seemed to shine a bright crimson. "Stephan, are you taking care of her?"

"We sure are, Brother Franklin. She'll stay with us until we find her a home." He gave her a quick pat on the shoulder. "She's no trouble at all."

"Sarah, I want to talk with you, please." He pointed a chubby finger toward the open back door. "Let's walk over by the tree."

"All right." She started for the old oak, wondering why he wanted to talk alone.

"Mary, I need a few private words with her. It won't take long."

"Take your time Brother Franklin, we'll wait by our carry-all."

The old preacher took long strides to where Sarah had squatted on her heels alongside the oak. She busied herself picking up acorns.

"Sarah, let's chat a moment."

She immediately stood, tall as her short body would allow and straight as an arrow. "Sure, what do you want to talk about?"

The girl liked Brother Franklin. Her mother had as well. He had visited Rachel and Sarah regularly on his way through the county.

"I want to ask you a question. If you don't know what I'm talking about, simply say so. However, if you do know, please tell me. I want you to trust me. Will you?"

"Yes, Brother Franklin."

Sarah thought it might be a Bible question to see what she knew. Or, maybe he wanted to know if the time had come for her to confess the Lord and be baptized in the river. What he asked, she did not expect. It left her speechless.

His eyes were warm, yet anxious. He delivered the question, and it hit her like a bolt of lightning from a thunderhead. "Sarah, did the 'packages' arrive at your house?"

The question knocked the wind from Sarah. For a moment her

mind blanked, and she felt as though she had landed flat on her back after falling from the giant tree. Her breath would not start.

The "packages!" How does he know? Only Mama and I call the run-away slaves "packages."

Sarah's eyes grew big, and her mouth dropped open. She could not even force out a peep.

*It's our secret, only ours! No . . ."*Packages?" The word finally swooshed from her in one big breath.

"Two packages set out from Darke County early last week. Did Rachel received them and forward them on?" A straightforward and blunt question, he anxiously awaited her answer. *If she knows, she'll tell me. She won't lie.*

The old man's deep-set eyes made her knees buckle as she met his gaze straight on. Words again caught in her throat.

I can trust him. Mama always spoke well of him. He's a man of God, like Papa.

Getting her legs under her, and once again standing straight, she started her answer, "Yes . . ."

"Preacher!" A loud, guff voice, sounding like it came straight from the flames of the Devil's pit, cut her short. "You, old man!"

Brother Franklin and Sarah turned to face two men leading their horses toward them. The tall man had dark scraggly hair and untrimmed lamb chop sideburns. The older man wore his hair long, and sported a pointy gray beard that rested on his chest.

These were the two at Mama's funeral. I know what they do, and they're up to no good.

The old brother said friendly with a kindly tone, "May I help you?" He really didn't think he could, but he wanted to be polite.

"Well, let's just see if you can," Graybeard growled. He sneered at them, and the girl noticed tobacco juice run from the corner of his mouth. "Have you seen two Nigras – a black, named Joseph, and his old wife, Polly? I know you Quakers hide runaways! Where you keeping them, preacher?"

Sarah stood two feet from the slave catchers, and she cared nothing for the experience. Slave hunters had ridden through before, sometimes visited the farm, but always spoke to Rachel. The girl remained inside each time. Catchers called the Negroes by names her mother told her to never use. She remembered her mother saying, "Negroes are people like us."

Sarah's guess about these men, when she first saw them at the funeral, was right.

"Sir, let me answer you," the preacher began politely. "I prefer to call the black race, Negro. Number two, I'm not a Quaker. I don't have a religious label. I'm simply a Christian. And third, I don't know the folks you're talking about. But, to make sure you don't misunderstand me, wherever these two runaways by the names of Joseph and Polly are, I hope they make it to wherever they're going. No man should own another as he does an animal. Negroes are humans and should be treated as such."

"Amen, Brother Franklin," Mary shouted from the carry-all.

"You tell them, Preacher," Stephan chimed in as he moved toward the men.

Sarah now realized she could trust the old preacher since he stood up to the repulsive men.

"Look preacher, it's against the law to keep runaways," the old man snarled the warning, "and I don't need you a preaching at me. I'll call them what I want, and I ain't changing. Now, you better give them up!"

"Sir, I believe when it comes to freeing men, God's law is much higher than man's. I defer to God's. But, I've already told you, I know nothing of the whereabouts of the Negroes." His eyes twinkled mischievously. "You're welcome to search my saddle bags."

Sarah gave out a timid laugh, and then covered her mouth.

"Little girl, what you laughin' about? Do you know about these two no-goods? Where do these Quakers or Christians, whatever you want to call them, where do they hide the runaways? You better not lie to me little girl!" The man snapped his fingers in her face. "You lie and there will be the dickens to pay. You know that ol' devil will git you!"

A shudder ran through the girl, while a bitter, awful fear tore at her insides. She backed away. The acorns slipped from her hand, disappearing into the grass. She never imagined the catchers turning on her.

What to do? Oh, what to do now! Mama told me to never answer a slave catcher's questions. They think I'm a little girl, good — my shortness works. "Don't say a word, Sarah, and they will think you know nothing. You're too little to throw in jail."

Reminding herself of her mother's instructions didn't matter at that moment. The fear that coursed through her small frame kept her silent.

"You fellows need to move out," Stephan Martin warned impulsively, stepping behind them. "Now we want no trouble here. This girl you're scaring half to death, with your foul speech and crude ways, lost her mother in an accident three days ago. She's staying with my wife and me. Neither she nor my family knows anything of the folks you're asking about. If we did, we wouldn't tell you." He pointed at the road. "Now, straddle your horses and get."

"Sorry, Miss, about your mother," the tall man spoke up.

"Aw, mount up, Joel," Graybeard ordered. Climbing astride his horse the old man rode north. The tall man followed close behind.

Immediately, Mary bee-lined it to Sarah, and wrapped her arms around the girl. Sarah bawled. Mary patted her shoulder and held her close, waiting for the girl to cry herself dry.

"They're gone now. Let's go on home," Mary spoke sweetly. "We'll fix a good dinner."

Nodding, Sarah turned to leave. She still had not given the preacher an answer. So, after getting herself where she could talk, Sarah whispered in Mary's ear, "Ask Brother Franklin to dinner, please."

Mary gave her a wry smile. "We invited him before preaching. He accepted."

While Mary, Jane, and Martha bustled about to put dinner on the table, Sarah and the preacher took a short stroll to a canebrake east of the house. When out of earshot, the girl spoke up.

"Brother Franklin," she whispered loudly, "the packages did arrive, and they're still at the house."

The old preacher gave Sarah a warm smile. "Do you know where the next station is located?"

"Yes, it's northeast about five miles. I've been before, once by myself."

He shook is head, amazed at her maturity. "Little girl, you keep on surprising me. I know the place, also."

"Those poor folks need food. I must go over there after dinner." Looking into his old lined face, she begged, "Will you help me?"

"Of course I will. Don't you worry over those two. They've come a long way out of the South. I'm sure they've been in worse tights. We'll make sure they eat and are moved along the railway. Sarah, you're a mighty fine girl. Your mother would be proud of you."

"She is proud of me. She knows when I do good things because God tells her!"

Puzzled by the remark, but smiling, the white haired gentleman nodded in agreement.

6

Safe House

As the group crossed the bridge Sarah spied two horses near the house. It sent a wave of fear through her. Looking over at the preacher, she thought on his decision to tell the Martins about the Underground Railroad. After dinner he had discussed it with Stephan and Mary, and they agreed to help – this time. She hoped they would decide to become agents. She wanted to continue her mother's work, but she needed help.

She wanted something else, too – a family. Of course, having her mother alive and home was really what she wanted. Sarah could not imagine life without her. Suddenly, a quick smile crossed her face. *Mama wouldn't want to come back now. She's in Heaven with my daddy, and they have no more troubles, no more slave catchers.*

The thought of the rough men sent a shiver down her spine. *No, I couldn't ask Mama to come back, even if it was possible. Heaven is too wonderful. Oh, Lord, help me to find a new family. That's my wish, just a family that will love me. Folks that will help me with Mama's work.*

As they pulled up out front, Graybeard appeared from the side.

"Well, if it ain't the preacher comin' to meet the lazy runaways. We know them no-goods are here, and we intend to root them out. Open the door," the man roared his command, "We're goin' inside!"

"Do you have the proper paperwork to make such a demand?" The preacher poked a finger at the slave hound. "This house is not open to the likes of you." His face became more crimson than usual, and the anger clearly began to build. "Paperwork please, or leave these premises, you're trespassing."

The slave catcher slowly reached into his pocket and pulled out a piece of paper.

"Here's my authority, mister!" He shoved it in Brother Franklin's face.

The old preacher pored over the official looking document and handed it to Stephan.

"I read your paper, sir. It gives you authority to capture slaves for a Mr. Reed. I guess you can do all the capturing you want outside of this property. You have no authority here."

"Now look here, preacher, if I think slaves are hiding in this house, I don't even need that paper you seem to think is so all-fired important." He brought his hand to rest on the holstered gun. "This pistol gives me all the authority I need."

The old fellow faced him head on. "Are you threatening me?"

Graybeard's icy voice filled the air, loud enough to echo off the barn. "I'm telling you if it takes shooting you to get inside this house, I'll shoot you doornail dead!"

Whether the catcher bluffed, or meant it, no one knew. With hand on the gun, he stared daggers at the preacher. Not to be stared down, the old "soldier of the cross" went eyeball to eyeball with the slaver.

"I see your business is more important to you than the laws of this state, or more importantly the laws of God. Now, you threatened to kill me. I'm a Christian, an old one at that. I trust the Lord's promise that when I die I'm going to Heaven. So, if you think by threatening me you're scaring me, you're wrong, sir. You can't threaten me with going to Heaven."

The big tough suddenly realized he could not bully the old man. As he considered his next move, the tall man emerged from the side yard.

"They ain't in the barn." His face gave one big sour look. "I pitch-forked the hay, too. Didn't stick nobody. Seen another little barn behind the house. Looks like they keep a horse and carriage in there. Didn't find nothin.' Maybe the blacks stole them and ran."

Gathering her courage, Sarah spoke up. "No one stole them. The buggy is at Mr. Carter's for repair, and Blackie is at the livery."

"I told you fellas her mother died in a buggy accident the other day," Stephan said, irritably.

"So, this is the little girl's place. Nobody living here right now, well – 1 -1, I bet them runaways are right inside making themselves to home. Now look here, you people," he thundered, "either you open the door or get it kicked in!"

Sarah jumped from the carriage and ran up the front steps. Carrying her mother's handbag she reached inside pulling out the key. She knew Joseph and Polly were in the hiding place, because the slave catcher did not find them in the carriage barn. Pushing the door open she scooted quickly across the room and hugged the small bookcase. Within seconds the men entered on the heels of the preacher and the Martins.

"Pull up all the rugs in the house!" Graybeard ordered. "These Quakers have trap doors and will hide blacks under the floor."

"We aren't Quakers," Sarah corrected him, her fear gone.

The men searched the kitchen area, one small bedroom, and the front sitting room where the bookcases stood. Looking under the bed for a trap door and not finding one, they pulled the quilt and sheets from the bed.

"No one under the mattress, let's get upstairs. Whoa, look!" Graybeard pointed out the window.

Immediately the girl felt her throat tighten and her heart race. *Are they running across the pasture?*

Tall Man stepped to the window and peeked out. "What ya see?"

"A door to a cellar on the side of the house. Did you look in there?"

"Of course I did! You think I'm stupid. Weren't nothin' but fruit and vegetables. A handful of crocks on the shelves. That's it."

"You search for trap doors and moveable rocks that lead underneath the house?"

"Look here old man," he barked. "I've been a chasin' slaves longer than you. I got you into this business. I know all their tricks. Shut up, and let's git upstairs! Probably be a hidden closet in one of them rooms."

The men stomped up, searched each room, and within minutes they returned.

"Where's the ladder?" Graybeard demanded, and he wasn't gentle about it.

With a voice calm and smooth as a mountain lake, Sarah replied, "The ladder is in the wood shed."

Almost immediately Tall Man returned with the ladder. Sarah glared at the bounty hunter, and his granite hard face sent another chill through the girl. *This man could be dangerous.*

"We've found the hiding place, Preacher, and your lazy slave friends will be caught shortly." Turning sharply, he stomped up the stairs again.

Brother Franklin looked over at Sarah with alarm. Stephan wrapped his arm around his shaking wife, drawing her close. She cried freely, her head on his shoulder.

"The ceiling of the upstairs hallway has a little door." Then, Sarah smiled big, knowing what they would find. "Three or four trunks are stored in the attic, nothing else."

Shortly the men reappeared. They brushed past the girl and tromped out the door.

Stephan followed, shouting at them from the front porch. "You fellas didn't put the ladder back in the woodshed."

"Aw, git inside, mister." Tall Man pulled his gun and pointed it at him. His face was stiff and cold. "Don't you ever, don't you ever, get in our way again. You do, and you'll be takin' a dirt nap."

Stephan moved back and ducked inside. The men wheeled their horses and rode north.

"Stephan! Are you trying to get yourself killed! Don't provoke them."

"They're bullies, Mary."

"Dangerous bullies!"

"I'll give the sheriff a report," the preacher promised. "They didn't have a warrant to search this house or property. They're lawless bounty hunters."

"I'll go with you. They sure were impolite." Stephan broke into a grin. "They didn't even introduce themselves."

Mary did not like his dark humor, and his remark only riled her more. Brother Franklin seeing trouble brewing between the two, changed the subject.

"Sarah, where have you hidden the packages?"

The statement caught the woman's attention, and she turned her eyes from Stephan. "The packages?" Mary squinted in thought, now forgetting her anger.

"Polly and Joseph. Mama called the slaves packages."

"Oh." Mary nodded, not really sure of it.

"Mary, the Underground Railroad is extremely secretive," the preacher spoke up. "The conductors try hard to keep the slave catchers off the trail of runaways. Agents always watch what they say to anyone because someone unfriendly to slaves might hear. At times they use code words such as 'packages.' Remember, you told me you didn't know Rachel had been helping slaves."

"I hardly believe it!" Mary caught her breath. "Rachel, a widow woman with a young child, worked alone?"

"When Eli and Rachel settled here they became agents. I have known of their work for many years. Sometimes I helped them secret slaves toward the North. So little is said, I didn't know if Sarah helped her mother or not. Rachel never mentioned it, and I didn't ask."

Sarah giggled. "I didn't know about Brother Franklin, either. Mama never told me. I've only known about the hiding place since I was seven."

"Now, about that hiding place, little girl, let's get those folks. Let them eat the fried chicken and biscuits Miss Mary brought."

"Right now, Brother Franklin." *He always calls me little girl. I guess old folks think anyone younger is little.*

Sarah turned and took the flower vase off the top shelf, placing it on the other bookcase. Again she removed the books and laid them on the floor. Stephan helped her. With the bookcase empty, Sarah asked Stephan to slide the case aside.

Disappearing into the kitchen, she called, "I'll be right back."

The preacher looked over and caught Mary's eye. They shrugged. Within seconds Sarah returned with the butcher knife.

Stephan's eyes bulged. "Whoa, young lady, what you doing with that knife?"

"Did you see the opening?"

The trap door set several feet from the window and that kept the area rather dark and hard to see. The group squinted intently at the floor. Finally Stephan whooped, "The wall!"

Sarah giggled and stuck the knife into the slit. After opening the little door she jerked the trapdoor and set it aside. With everyone peering at the opening she bent over into the darkness.

"Joseph, Polly, it's all right to come up."

After everyone introduced themselves, the preacher told the runaway slaves they were friends of Sarah. He explained what happened to Rachel and promised to move them after dark to the next station.

"Sarah, after these folks eat their dinner I want to look at the hiding place," Stephan suggested. "It looks quite interesting. Your daddy built this house didn't he?"

"Yes. Mama said he and Mr. Sam and Miss Eliza built it. They made the secret place to hide runaway slaves. He knew about the Underground Railroad in Ohio because Virginia had one, too."

Sarah glanced about at all of them. "Please keep this secret. I promised Mama to never tell anyone. No one can ever know. Mama said it's too dangerous. I've broken a promise, and now you know about the secret." She hung her head. Suddenly, she felt ashamed for betraying her promise to her mother. "I shouldn't have told. Please, give your word you won't tell!"

"Sarah, we promise," Stephan gestured with his hand. "We can see it's exceedingly dangerous. You and Rachel were brave to help the runaways."

"Sarah, your mother wrote in the letter you had a secret. She knew you were a good girl and wouldn't break the promise – unless you had to. It's all right." Mary tenderly touched the girl's arm. "You need help and so do the slaves. You've done the right thing and your mother would be pleased with you."

Her mouth smiled, but her heart still ached. "I miss Mama." Her face sagged so low it looked stepped on sideways. "I don't know what I'm going to do without parents." She clasped Mary tight and hung on, her body shaking with emotion. "What will I do?"

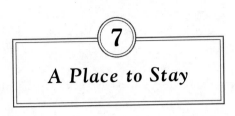

7

A Place to Stay

Arriving at the old lady's house, the doctor hopped from his buggy. He had come to pick up his baby boy. Doc's wife lay sick in bed – too ill to watch the little fellow, and Granny had agreed to keep the baby while he made his rounds.

"Granny, I sure appreciate your help while Elizabeth is ill. The baby give you any trouble?"

"He be a little fussy. Kept a pullin' at his ear."

Now, Granny doctored sick folks with herbs and all kinds of home-grown "cures." Many people in the county came to her when they were ailing. She had lived in the area much longer than the doctor, and folks trusted her.

"I cured him of it."

"You did?" Doc raised his eyebrows in doubt.

"Shore did. Fired up my ol' corncob pipe. After I had her a goin' good, I blew the smoke into the baby's ear, soft a course. Oh, he liked it right well – settled right down, no more fussin.'"

"Thank you, Granny." He winked. "I sure appreciate your good help."

"Aw, it be nuttin. Bring the little one anytime."

"I must hurry along."

"Doc, afore ya go, I kinder have sompun important to lay on ya. Got a minute?"

"For you, I do."

"Mary Martin be too weak and sickly to take on Sarah. Will ya go over there and tell Sarah to come live with me? I'll see the judge about makin' me her guardian."

"Granny Evans, this is wonderful news. I know Sarah loves you as if you were her own grandmother. It's a shame all of her grandparents have passed on. I believe she has an uncle, but no one knows were he lives."

"I met the skunk afore," she spat it out. "Hope he be gone fer good."

The old lady gave a dark look, something strange like Doc had never seen before. He decided to keep quiet. No sense in riling her further.

He headed the horse and buggy northeast toward the Martin's house. Doc arrived within minutes and several children rushed to the hitching post to greet him. He had delivered most of them. The kids escorted him all along the pathway. About then Mary appeared on the porch, waving. Her flour-streaked face gave away how she had spent her day.

"Dr. Baum, what a pleasant surprise." Mary swung the door open. "Come in this house."

"I can't stay. Elizabeth is ill and I need to go on, but I must speak with you. It won't take long."

Mary quickly descended the steps. "How's the baby?"

"He's doing well."

"A big boy isn't he?"

"Yes, he is." Doc returned to the buggy and set the baby on the seat. Turning around to face her straight on, he delivered the message. "I came by to tell you Granny wants to keep Sarah."

The woman stood speechless, staring at him. *I love Sarah, yet I can barely handle my own brood,* she told herself. *And now – Stephan wants to take on Rachel's work. It's all too much at once.*

"Dr. Baum," she finally got the words out, "this is so kind of Granny." She sniffled. "I know Rachel and Eli would be happy if they knew. Why didn't Granny come tell us?"

"She's a little afraid Sarah wouldn't want to stay with her. I think she wanted the girl to decide without Granny standing here. Let's tell, Sarah!" He pointed toward the house. "I believe she'll want to go."

Gathered on the porch the family tried hard to hear. Pointing to Sarah, Mary motioned with her hand.

Sarah pointed a finger at herself saying, "Me?"

"Yes, Sarah – hurry!"

Jake, the youngest son, taunted in a singsong voice, "Sarah is in trouble."

Making a fast turn, she gawked at him and made a face.

"Naw, she ain't, Jake," Harold, the oldest took his turn to heckle. "The doc is gonna give her a big spoonful of ba-a-a-d tastin' medicine."

Mr. Martin warned the boys to leave her alone. "Looks as though Doc wants to talk with her, probably check her arm."

Although her face may have told otherwise, she replied, "They don't bother me, Mr. Martin." Then, before he could reply, she raced down the steps.

"What, Mrs. Martin? Is something wrong at the farm? Did something happen to the run. . . ." She clapped a hand over her mouth.

Immediately Mary glanced to Doctor Baum, and then told Sarah not to worry about the farm.

"What were you about to say?" Doc picked up his crying baby. "I didn't hear over the racket," he smiled a wry smile.

"Uh, well – I'm hoping, that is – I want my animals cared for." She peeked sideways at Mary. "I think about them everyday."

Something in her voice doesn't match what she said, Doc thought to himself.

"Sarah, we have something to tell you," Mary rushed on.

The girl's eyes grew big, and she held her breath. Then, Doc gave her the good news. She would have her own room, and chores would be assigned to her. For a while she would be Granny's granddaughter. She would have a home.

For a brief moment Sarah looked startled. As she thought it over, everyone remained quiet.

Repeating his words, her voice barely above a whisper, she eked out, "Stay at Granny's house?"

"It'll be your home until new parents are found."

Her face colored up pretty, and light danced in her big brown eyes.

"Yes!" she shrieked. "Yes! But . . . only 'til my new parents come. It won't be long. I know it. I just know it."

"Granny said you may stay as long as it takes."

"Hoora-a-a-a-y! I won't be a bother. I'll be good – I promise."

Mary stooped to hug the girl, and Sarah wrapped her arms about her neck. She whispered something only Mary could hear. The woman nodded her head in agreement and then whispered back to Sarah. The look of gladness on the girl's face had erased the worry of moments before.

"Granny will come before dinnertime tomorrow. Have your things ready to go."

"I'll be ready, Doctor. I sure will."

8

The Drying Shed

"Can you walk home with me?" Martha asked.

"No, I'm waiting on Granny," said Sarah. Both girls dawdled in swings outside the schoolhouse, talking of things all twelve year olds go on about. "She has business at the wheelwright's and the apothecary. Do you want to go with us?"

"I want to, but I have to get home to do my chores. I'll see you at meeting on Sunday. Bye."

"Bye, Martha, see you Sunday."

Sarah pushed backward and pulled her feet up. The cooling breeze against her face felt refreshing on the hot summer day. Watching the barn swallows take flight from the eves of the school reminded her of the farm. Those amazing birds, sailing high above, then dipping, turning, wings completely still, slicing the air effortlessly. They brought back a flood of memories.

Her mind wandered to thinking about the previous spring – before her mother went to Heaven. At the farm Rachel pushed her in the swing that hung from the old elm tree, and the girl would pretend to be a bird in flight. Yelling for her mother to push harder, she flew as high as the swing allowed. Oh, how she longed for those days. If only she could go back. Go back in time – before the snake, that evil snake.

Her lips curved down, "I miss you, Mama."

Swinging back and forth she pondered thoughts an orphan girl often imagines. She did not remember her daddy, but her mother's laughter still rang in her ears, reminding her of things past. She no longer heard her mother's greeting at the front door, and no longer felt her mother's hands pushing her higher and higher as she flew through the air on the swing.

I wish I had parents, she daydreamed. *I like my friend, Martha, and I love Granny, but it's not the same. I hate being an orphan!*

"Sarah Smith, hey there girl – are ya a hearin' me?"

"Huh? Oh – Granny!" She forced a weak smile. "I've been thinking about something."

"Ya ready to go? We be burnin' daylight sittin' here." The old lady grinned sideways, barely enough to show her teeth.

Jumping from the swing, she grabbed her knapsack and ran. Climbing into the buggy, Sarah plopped onto the seat. With eyes straight ahead she mimicked Granny. "What ya waitin' on – let's cut dirt!" Quickly, her face broke into a toothy smile.

Granny stared, one eye shut. The old lady's face drew up as though she had eaten a sour pickle. The silence continued, neither giving an inch. Finally, Sarah turned her head ever so slowly until she locked onto Granny's face. The girl's eyes widened, pushing her dark eyebrows up, and then her laughter rolled. Within seconds, a slight smile lifted one corner of the old lady's mouth, and she pulled the girl close with a tight hug.

As the buggy drew to a stop in front of the wheelwright's, Sarah jumped out. Racing into the building she greeted the craftsman.

"Hello, Sarah. I haven't talked with you since last winter when Rachel had that wagon wheel repaired. Oh, I'm sorry! I didn't mean to bring to mind hurtful things. I'm sorry about your mother."

"Mr. Carter, remembering Mama isn't hurtful." Her face glowed just talking about it. "Mama is in Heaven with my daddy. Someday I'll see them."

"You sure will." The man patted her back. "Granny Evans, how are you this fine day? Did this young lady come with you?"

"Shore she did. She be a stayin' with me fer awhile. Ya got the wagon wheel done? I need to git that there wagon of mine back in use."

"I'm working on it now. Be done shortly. I'll fetch it over later and put it on your wagon."

"I'll put it on myself. Jist deliver it to my front door – the rest I can handle."

"Now, Granny, you need help . . ."

"Look here, mister, I ain't a needin' no help. I'm strong as an ox and can lick my weight in wildcats. If I need help, ye'll be the first to know."

He shrugged his shoulders. "All right, Granny."

"Is this the wheel?" Sarah asked.

"Sure is, Miss."

"What are those?" She pointed to several curved pieces of wood.

"Fellies."

"What's a felly? Why's there a hole in it? What goes in the hole? What . . ."

"Slow down, Miss Sarah. Let me show you." The wheelwright picked up a round piece of wood. "See this hub with the holes in it?"

"Uh huh."

"I made this hub, and cut these holes, called 'mortises.' I'll hammer fourteen spokes into the mortises around each hub. Let me show you."

He tapped the first spoke into the hub. It fit so tight it could not be pulled out. He continued to tap in several more.

"Now I see," Sarah squealed. "The felly goes on the other end of the spoke."

The man grinned big. Taking one of the curved pieces of wood, he hammered it onto the spoke. The tendon went all the way through the felly, but stopped even with the other side.

"This is how it's done." He tapped another into place and asked the girl if she wanted to try. She did. "I'll do the rest the same way, and when finished the wheel will be round. Afterwards, I'll cover the rim with a 'strake.'"

"The iron thing?" Once more Sarah pointed, this time to a finished wheel leaning against the wall.

"Yes, the blacksmith makes it and puts it on the wheel when it's very hot. Then he cools it with cold water."

"I know why," the girl jumped in.

"Tell us what yer a thinkin,'" Granny said.

"When the iron becomes cold it shrinks, and the strake tightens onto the wheel."

The wheelwright glanced at Granny. "She's a smart one, got an old head on young shoulders." He gave her a wink. "She could make a good school marm someday."

"Yes!" she started to jump, and then caught herself, attempting to act more ladylike. "I am. Someday – that's what I plan to be. Isn't that right, Granny?"

"Shore nuff. Ya want to teach – so there ain't nuttin' gonna be a stoppin' ya," Granny agreed, crossing her arms. She appeared to dare anybody to disagree. "Ya can be what yer a mind to be, and the men cain't keep ya from it."

Sarah took a turn with the hammer, driving a felly in place. She liked it for learning something new, but she wouldn't want to do it for a living. Of course, she understood girls certainly couldn't be wheelwrights, blacksmiths or even a barber. But she could and would be a schoolteacher. That had always been her wish. So, now she had two wishes. A new family must come first, and soon. Already twelve, she would be marrying age in three or four years.

"Granny, I'll bring this wheel to your place in two hours. Be glad to help you put it on." He gave a slight wave of the hand. "No extra charge."

"No! I can do it myself. Now ya leave it out front like I asked. Don't be doin' nuttin' else," her voice took on a peculiar tone. "I can handle it."

The man could not make out Granny's stubbornness. He shook his head.

"Sarah, let's cut dirt. We have to go by Mr. Balzer's place afore we go home. Ya ready to git?"

"Sure am!" She made a dash for the buggy. Hopping up and settling into the seat, she cracked, "Let's hurry – we be burnin' daylight!"

"Sarah, I want ya to help ol' Granny with her herbs and potions. I need to re – supply my medicine box."

"Hoora-a-a-a-y! I like helping with the herbs," Sarah screamed, acting more like eight than twelve.

The old lady covered her ears. "Put a cork in that there yellin'. Ya keep that up, I might have to fetch a knot on yer noggin."

"Oops, sorry, Granny. Shhh, I forgot." She put a finger to her lips.

Suddenly, her voice took a strange turn – at least it sounded strange for a young lady. "Yes, Miss Evans, I must act like a lady," she spoke quietly, putting her nose in the air. "Ma'am, may I gather herbs from the garden, Ma'am? It would be sooo lovely to help with the cuttings," the girl said, in a breathy voice with a snooty tone.

"Sarah girl, are ya makin' fun? What be that new voice I jist heared. Sounded pert near like a high-toned fancy woman talkin.'"

"Yes, Mum, by all means it was fancy talk." Sarah broke up laughing at her attempt to mimic some of the high society women who belonged to the local garden club.

Granny laughed along with her. She enjoyed a good joke, and Sarah was a jokester.

Then, the old lady took up where she left off. "Cain't use most of them straight from the garden. I dry them first. Remember what I taught ya?"

"I remember." Her voice returned to normal. "We have to get them from the drying shed. Let's go," she shouted, racing outside.

Granny followed behind, walking at a steady pace. Entering the shed the old lady found Sarah waiting by the long table, the work spot where the she stripped leaves from stems to use in her tonics, potions and teas. After stripping the leaves she would take them inside to her dinning table. There, she crushed them into powders and placed them into bottles.

Granny organized her work and knew exactly what needed doing. She had learned from her mother. Many of the new things she had learned, Mr. Balzer, the apothecary, had taught her. She gathered many of the plants, berries, roots, and bark from the area around Wapakoneta. Granny's business included selling part of her "gatherings" to the apothecary. As the old lady traded at the drugstore, Mr. Balzer would tell her what he knew about doctoring people.

"Granny, tell me again about these herbs and plants? I can't remember. Look at all of these! What's this green one? What kind of bark is this? What's this liquid in the jar? How long do you dry the herbs? What's . . ."

"Sarah Smith!" The girl jumped back from the table. "How in tarnation can I answer a question when ya keep a jawin.' Now I cain't remember the first question 'cause of the others."

The old lady smiled, and Sarah knew Granny meant no harm.

"Oops, I only want to learn new things." Slowly, she pronounced each word. "What . . . is . . . in . . . the . . . jar?"

"Yer becomin' a real clown, ain't ya girl?" Not waiting for an answer, "That there be lamp oil."

"I don't see a lamp in here." Sarah looked the shed over, top to bottom.

"Naw, that ain't fer no lamp. I use it in my doctorin.'"

Sucking her breath real hard, she blew out, "Do your patients drink it?" Her eyes became saucer big.

"Tarnation! No! I ain't tryin' to kill them. Oh, guess it would git rid of their ailment all right – but it be a mite too permanent, don't ya think?"

Sarah burst out laughing, and pointed. "Granny, you're funny."

"Least ya dint call me funny lookin.' Listen up now! This here oil be fer a person's head."

"Lamp oil is put on a person's head?" she screeched, hardly believing it.

"Have ya ever had head bugs?"

"Head bugs? Nooooo, I don't think so. Head bugs . . ."

"Some folks call them lice. The little critters git in yer hair and hang on. Itch yer head sompun fierce." The thought of it had old lady scratching. "Well, lookit that. Jist a talkin' about it makes my old coconut itch."

"Coconut?"

"Shore, ya knowed – yer head."

"Oh."

"Have ya ever been called pumpkin head?"

"Noooo, I don't think so. Oh, Buford called me pumpkin brain one time."

"Nope, ain't the same. And, ya can tell Buford to stop his name callin'. It ain't nice. Don't let me hear my little Miss doin' it, either. Ya don't ever heared me callin' folks names, do ya?"

"Well, let's see, I think I heard you . . ."

"We ain't got time fer jawin'. Now, let me tell ya more about the head bugs. I . . ."

"I remember a long time ago I had bugs in my hair." The girl started up where they left off. "I don't remember what Mama called them."

"Long time ago?" Granny snorted. "Why yer only twelve years old. Couldn't been too long ago. Thirty, forty years ago – now that be a long time ago."

"Granny, twelve years is a long time for me." Sarah placed her hands on her hips. "It's . . . well, it's a lifetime!"

"Ha! Guess yer right about that one. Mr. Carter's right – yer a smart one. What did Rachel do fer yer head?"

"She cut all my hair off and shaved my head smooth. I looked like an old bald grandpa." She whispered loudly, "I barely remember it."

"Guess that got rid of them all right. No need to do that anymore. Not when a person uses Granny's sure – fire treatment. This be what I do to rid folks of the little varmints. I apply this here oil to their hair until it be soaked right good. Then, I wrap the head to keep the hair wet, and the oil from runnin' on the person's face and neck. I tell them to keep doin' this soaking two or three more times in the next 24 hours. Afterwards, they can wash with lye soap and then rench it clean. The lice and their nits will be gone." She gave Sarah a wink. "Granny's cure keeps them from losing their hair."

"Rench? You mean rinse it clean?"

"Shore, rench it clean."

Rubbing the top of her head, Sarah stared wide-eyed at the old lady. "Granny, that sounds like it gets rid of more than the lice. It might take your skin, too."

"Aw, it might take the first layer, but that be all." She looked Sarah straight in the eye. "It'll grow again soon enough."

The girl saw something in the old lady's eyes, but what? She was hard to figure. *Hmmmm. Doctor Baum told me Granny sometimes stretches the truth.*

Muffled sounds stirred the girl awake. Listening close, she picked out Granny's voice, but did not recognize the deep bass of the other. The closed door kept the words out. Slipping from bed, Sarah tiptoed toward the door. The voices faded.

They must have gone into the keeping room.

Leaving the lamp unlit, she opened the bedroom door and slowly eased her way along the wall, stopping at the top of the stairs. Still unable to hear the words clearly, she tried cupping her hand around her ear. The girl guessed right, they had moved into the other room. Stepping quietly and holding tight to the handrail, she nervously came downstairs. Sarah worked hard at keeping her movements silent.

Squeak! Instantly, she froze mid-step, not moving a muscle. Sarah listened close. The noise had not come from the stairs. With her ear cocked to one side, she again heard the same sound. It was the door being shut.

They're going out back. Why?

Reaching the bottom step, she waited, listening. They had left through the back door, but she could still faintly hear them. A candle sitting on the table dimly lit the dark. Sarah hated darkness and rushed along the short hallway to be near the light. Glancing about the keeping room she noticed everything appeared in place. Then, pulling on the knob, the girl cracked the back door. She squeezed through.

Whew! I didn't make any noise.

Two flickering lights moved without hurry toward the drying shed. She quietly followed at a distance. The girl shook with excitement, trying to remember what her friend Running Fox told her about tracking game. *Move silently – ever so silently.* She gained on them.

"Ya can stay in here tonight," Granny whispered loudly. "Got some nice soft hay on the floor. I'll be a gittin' that there wagon wheel on in the morning afore we eat our grub. Then we can git on to the next stop."

Crack! A branch split. Everyone stopped.

Oh, Sarah! What did you step on? She dropped to the ground, trying to flatten out pancake thin.

"Ye there," Granny shouted, her voice clear. "Who in thunder be out there?" She pulled a gun from her knitting bag. "Ya better come over here in the light."

Sarah held her breath, afraid to breathe.

"Lookit here, whoever be out there, I'm a given ya to the count of three to come over here or I might be gittin' this here gun a smokin.' What it gonna be?"

"Granny," the soft voice floated in from the dark.

"Sarah Smith, what in tarnation! Git yerself over here outta the dark!"

"Don't shoot me," the squeaky voice cried out.

"I ain't a shootin' nobody – shore nuff not my house guest. Now git yer hide over here where I can lay eyeballs on ya."

Creeping slowly at first, Sarah finally moved close enough for Granny to see her. The girl raced to the old lady and clutched her waist. She cried.

"What be all the bawling about?" Granny patted her back. "I warn't really gonna fire off this here cannon." She laughed big. "I jist want to see what I'm a gunnin' fer. Besides, I ain't never fired a gun unless there be a need." The old lady's blue eyes twinkled in the candlelight, and Sarah relaxed a bit. "I guess I can pert near hold my own in bluffin' folks."

"I'm sorry, Granny. I didn't mean to spy. I'm afraid of the dark and want stay near you." Her voice choked with emotion. "Don't leave me, I'm afraid of noises in the dark."

"I ain't about to leave ya. Ol' Granny be right here with ya, and don't ya be a fergittin,' the Good Lord be always alongside. Don't ya knowed He sends His angels to look over ya. No, no way yer alone. Yer Mammy ever taught ya the Twenty-third Psalm?"

"Uh huh," she grunted. "The Lord is my Shepherd. I know it. Mama said it often. Sometimes I forget to remember it." Sarah sniffled and wiped her eyes on her nightshirt.

"What? That there be sompun ol' Granny would say."

Sarah giggled and squeezed her tighter. "Who were you talking to?"

Granny looked around, but the man had disappeared. "Well, I'll be a horn-toad. Where did he go? He be a feller jist a passin' through. Let's see if he got scared and hid out."

Holding the candle out to light the way, the old lady and girl entered the shed.

9

Help from the Indian

Dawn came early, and Sarah was up with the first rooster crow. After breakfast she and their visitor helped Granny secure the wheel to the wagon. With that job done and after finishing the other chores, they were off.

Scatterings of hay lazily fell as the wagon jolted along the road east of town. Sitting in the narrow seat beside the old lady, Sarah chattered away.

"Ohhhh!" Granny yelped.

The girl stopped her talk and took notice. "Something wrong?"

"Jist felt a chill go through me, and seein' how it be summer an' all, I think maybe somebody jist stepped on my grave."

"Granny, you don't believe that old saying, do you?"

"Cain't rightly say fer shore, but I ain't sick none, and today be hot, hot as the front door hinges on the devil's house. So, might be sompun to it."

"Buford told the girls at school that a chill in the summer means something bad will happen before the month is out."

"How much stock ya gonna put in what Buford goes on about? Not much I be a thinkin.' I jist keep a believin' in what I believe, at least until it be proved different.

"Take a gander up that way." Granny pointed up the road.

Sarah tugged her bonnet down to shade her eyes. They faintly heard a man cursing, and saw a horse lying on the road. Coming alongside, Granny pulled on the reins. Grabbing her knitting bag, she placed it in her lap and slipped her hand inside.

63

"Git up ya lazy no good," the man yelled his demand.

It was Graybeard, and he pounded the poor horse unmercifully with a rope.

"Hey there, Mister."

The tone of Granny's voice caused Sarah to snap her head sideways. She saw the look on the old lady's face, a look mean enough to scare a big snake.

"Lighten up on the horse beatin.' I don't hold to cussing, neither."

"It's my horse, I own him. I'll beat him if I want! And – talk like I want, too." Ugliness and anger shot from his cold eyes, not a person to be taken lightly. "It's none of your business, old lady."

"I'm a makin' it my business." She turned up the heat in her fiery eyes. "Cain't ya see the horse be ailing? Now, leave him be."

The slave catcher's voice – and look – brought fear to Sarah's heart. Her insides quivered, and she scooted even closer to Granny, grabbing her arm.

"Ah, yes!" He hissed. The evil sound would have scared the horns off the devil. "I see my little curly headed friend is with you today. You going to visit your farm? Maybe help a runaway?"

Her mouth went dry, her heart thudded in her chest, but she kept quiet.

"Not talking today?" His tone revealed he took great pleasure taunting her. "You're hurting my feelings."

Granny had no problem talking. She fired back. "Slave catcher ain't got no feelins, does he?"

Ignoring the old lady, Graybeard again yelled curse words at the fallen horse. The animal remained on the ground, refusing to stand. Once more the slave catcher raised his arm to beat the animal.

"Ho!"

Glancing up, the bounty hunter saw Zeke, the town's stonecutter. He reined up behind Granny. The old fellow slowly climbed from his wagon and walked to the fallen horse. Stooping to one knee, he rubbed the animal's nose, and whispered gently in its ear.

"Don't touch the horse! Get outta the way or I'll lash you along with this lazy no good animal. You're not gonna put your black hands on my property."

Zeke raised his head, and stared eye to eye with Graybeard. "The Good Book says, 'A righteous man regardeth the life of his beast.' This horse is sick. You keep that up, and you be killin' him."

"This is none of your affair, colored boy. You may be a freed slave, but that gives you no right to be sassin' a white man. Now you git on your wagon and leave. Do it now, boy!"

Shaking his head at the insult of being called a boy, Zeke stood and started for his wagon. Sarah held to Granny even tighter, and the old lady put her arm around the girl.

"What's in the wagon, boy? I'm lookin' for a big black." He hurried to the rear of Zeke's wagon. "I think maybe he's under that mound of hay."

"I'm on my way to the cemetery with a headstone. That's my business. The hay is to rest the headstone on." Zeke shrugged. "I don't know nuthin' of a colored man."

"Sure you don't." Graybeard gave out his evil laugh. Pulling a long blade knife from his belt he stabbed into the hay on Zeke's wagon. "Let's jist see how long before I hit flesh." After circling the wagon and finding nothing, he turned abruptly and shouted at Granny. "Old lady, let's be lookin' in that hay on your wagon. Wouldn't put it past you haulin' a slave in there." Raising his knife to continue the search, he never brought it down. In the quiet country air, everyone heard the sound. Granny had pulled from her bag and cocked the biggest gun Sarah had ever laid eyes on.

"Let's not be a lookin' in that hay, mister." Granny lowered the gun until the barrel pointed directly at Graybeard's neck. "Now ye may be thinkin' yer gonna push an old man and lady around, but I got news fer ya. Ya ain't. Ya ain't even ain't. Now git on down the road, enjoy the walk to town. We'll take care of the animal."

Granny's eyes narrowed, dark and brooding. She watched his every move. The slave catcher's eyes flared with anger, he knew he had lost the battle. Deciding to quit and go, he trudged off, murmuring a curse on everyone.

Whether the old lady would really have shot him, no one knew – not even Granny. Full of bluster, she sounded meaner than a country dog. Yet, actually hurting someone, even the slave catcher, no one could say. Hopefully she would never have to find out. Granny believed in the Lord's ways; and she didn't want to hurt anyone. Talking big, and acting tough had to be done sometimes, just to keep bad people from hurting the good. The gun was for show, and she prayed to God it always would be.

"Is he going to die?" Sarah asked anxiously, eyeing the fallen horse.

"Hard to say, little one," Zeke offered. "I'll stay and water him and pull my wagon alongside to shade him, maybe he'll come around. The stone can wait."

"Yer a good man, Zeke."

Staring into the distance, Granny waited for Graybeard to disappear over a rise in the road. Waiting several more minutes, she finally turned and hurried to her wagon.

"Jim," she spoke in a low voice. "Stay covered, we be at the next station soon. It ain't far."

Zeke looked over at the old lady. He quickly realized a runaway lay hidden beneath the hay. "Bless you, Granny."

She winked at the stonecutter, while Jim remained silently buried in the wagon. Graybeard had lost this time, but he would return. Slave catchers did not give up easily.

Breaking into the sunlight the little wagon moved toward the old Indian's log house. Spotting Running Fox on the front porch, Sarah waved. Running Fox stopped his wood carving, and the old bronzed face brightened with a big smile.

"Granny Evans, how are you today? Many moons have come and gone since you have been out here." He chuckled. "You looking for someone to nurse?"

"Hello, Indian. It's been a while, fer shore. Let me tell ya sompun.

I don't need yer business. I'm busier than a tall farmer fightin' three snakes with a short stick. Ya still using that old quack Medicine Man? He'll be yer death if ya keep usin' him."

"Don't use him, Granny. I call on Dr. Baum, or simply treat myself. I know a little about herbs and roots." His eyes twinkled. "Sarah, have you come to play in the meadow?"

Her face clouded and her lips thinned out. "We have business, sir."

"Oh, you do. This sounds serious." He returned her stern look. "What kind of business do you have with the old Indian?"

Jumping from the wagon she knocked on the side. "Mr. Jim! Mr. Jim! It's all right."

The hay stirred. The big man stood, and the dry hay flew everywhere.

"This is Mr. Jim," her eyes pled for understanding. "He needs your help."

Running Fox gave the runaway slave a blank-face look. The old Indian nodded slightly, yet his expression never changed.

"Sir, I'm sorry. I didn't want to tell anyone you helped slaves, but Mr. Jim needs help. I . . ."

"Let's go inside," he cut her off.

Closing the door, Running Fox pointed, and everyone took a seat at the dinning table.

"I didn't know Granny helped slaves," Sarah picked up where she left off, "but she does! Granny told me she doctors the hurting and takes them out to the farm. I knew she sometimes came to doctor runaways, but I didn't know she's an agent, too.

"Mr. Jim can't go there – the slave catchers keep watch. They ride near the farm all the time. They know we help slaves, but haven't been able to prove it." Her eyes filled with tears. "I told Granny! I know you and I had a secret. We made a pact to never tell. Mama and I had a secret, too. But, Brother Franklin showed me sometimes you have to share the secret if it helps people." The tears began to stream her cheeks. "Now, I have broken two promises, the one I made to Mama and the one to you."

Quickly Jim spoke, "I sorry, Miss Sarah. Dint mean to gives you hurt. I just wants to be free."

"I'm not hurt, Mr. Jim." She sniffled.

"Now, let me say sompun."

The Indian raised his hand and waved the old lady off. His face was quiet – unreadable.

"Sarah, the old preacher is right." Running Fox nodded his agreement. "Sometimes the good of others is more important than a promise. We should not take promises lightly, but when freedom and lives are at stake, a person has no other choice. You did the right thing." He touched her shoulder. "Besides, Granny knows I keep runaways here."

"I know, Granny told me, but I still broke a promise."

"You did the right thing, you thought of Jim and keeping him safe. If you were a Shawnee, you would be an honored brave."

Wiping tears with the back of her hand, she made her face smile, glad in her heart he understood.

"It's about dinner time. You folks hungry?"

"We be hungry all right," Granny told him. "Ain't had food since early morning. Fact be, I'm so hungry my stomach thinks my mouth be sewed shut."

"Let's put dinner together," the old Indian offered. "Little girl, why don't you go and pull several green onions, and pick a few tomatoes from the garden. Hurry along while we start in here."

"I'm on my way," Sarah yelled over her shoulder, streaking through the doorway.

"Whew! That girl is always in a rush. She goes at things like she's fighting a bear with a hickory switch." Running Fox opened the old pine cupboard. "Granny, pull that crock . . ."

"Granny! Granny!" Sarah's scream shook everyone to the core. Not her ordinary loudness, this told of an urgent, fearful something. "Granny," she gasped, flying through the door. "Two men! I saw them ride out of the trees. The sheriff, and that terrible man on the road. Oh, Mr. Jim, they're after you! I know it! I know it!"

"Quick!" the Indian said urgently, pointing at the hearthstone. "Help me move it, Jim."

Taking hold, Running Fox started to shove, giving out a hoarse groan. Jim grabbed a corner with his shovel of a hand, and moved it with ease. They pushed it aside barely enough for the slave to slip through. The Indian pointed into the black of the hole.

"Down there quick! Sorry – no time to light a candle. The ladder is short."

The runaway squeezed through the opening in the floor and moved down the ladder. Running Fox motioned to Granny and Sarah for help in sliding the stone in place.

Bang! Bang! Bang! The pounding shook the door, and rattled Sarah's nerves.

"Hey! Half-breed! Open this door."

"It's Graybeard!" Sarah screeched, a look of terror froze her face.

"Let's push, don't quit now," groaned the old man. The stone slipped in place, and Sarah lay flat against it, about to burst with tears.

Bang! Bang! Bang! The pounding started up again.

"Sarah, get yourself together – and now!" Running Fox ordered with a loud whisper, and not real gentle about it. "You act like nothing's wrong. Sit on this rock and sit straight. We have a man to save!"

Graybeard slammed the door with his boot. "Open up old man, or I'm kicking it in."

"Back off, mister." The second man's voice came from outside. "The Indian is slow."

Opening the door, Running Fox stared hard into the catcher's eyes. Neither blinked.

"I have a warrant to search this cabin, Running Fox." The sheriff held up an official looking document. "Sorry, but I have to abide the law. This man has certified papers to capture a colored man named Jim and return him to his owner. Is there a slave in this house?"

The bronzed man kept his eyes locked on the bounty hunter, neither would give. Suddenly, the catcher in his gruff loud voice, started to fuss and kick about what he called a good-for-nothing Indian.

Running Fox finally answered the sheriff's question and never blinked. "No slave in this house." His eyes were cold as a grizzly's claw in winter.

"Sheriff," the slave catcher snapped, ignoring the Indian, "some of the boys have suspected this old Indian of hiding runaways for a long time. I know that big black is here, just like I told you. Grandma had him under that hay for sure, and they was headed north. Look over there." He pointed his crooked, unwashed finger. "That's her wagon and that old broken down horse of hers. Told you what I saw, and I'm right. Grandma is inside with her sweet little friend, and that slave boy. Indian, stand aside." He pushed on Running Fox, but it was like pushing on granite.

"Hold on," the sheriff grabbed the man's arm. "We're not walking over people to carry out our duty. Running Fox, you know me. I'm a fair man. But, these papers require me to assist this fellow. I'm an officer of the court, and it makes no never mind if I like it or not. So, let us come in."

The old Indian stood aside and silently watched the intruders enter his home. Graybeard immediately searched each room, pulling up rugs and generally disturbing the place. The sheriff refused to help. After searching the rooms, the attic, and around the house, the slave catcher ended up where Sarah sat on the hearth. She held two of Running Fox's animal carvings. Lifting her eyes to meet Graybeard's cold-eyed stare, she quickly glanced away.

"What you up to, little girl?" His eyes narrowed to dark slits. Curling his lip to a sneer, he accused her. "I know you're helping this half-breed, like you helped your mother."

The words sucked her breath away. She jerked her head up, and her mouth opened. No words, only thoughts were possible. *He knew Mama hid slaves! How?*

"Surprised I know about yer mama? Oh, I know all right. Been told yer daddy helped the runaways all the time. Yer mama helped, too. No reason to quit when he died." Graybeard let out his evil, bone-rattling laugh. "I bet you think just like her. Don't you girl?"

"Hey dullard, leave the girl alone." Granny got right up in his face. "She ain't got nuttin' to say, but I do."

"Is that so? Well, what is it, Grandma?"

"Leave!" Granny spat out the order as though she tasted poison. "Sooner yer gone, sooner we open the house, and air out the smell."

"Look here, Grandma, I don't . . ."

"Mister," the sheriff latched on to his elbow, "the search is over."

"I'm finished – today. But you believe me, Indian, you too, Grandma, I'm not finished with the likes of you. I know the slaves get help from you two, and the girl be doing her share of it, too. When I prove it, you're both heading to the jailhouse and paying a fine for breaking the Fugitive Slave Act. It's the law! And I'm thinking the little girl should be taken away from you lawbreakers. You're all a bad influence on her. Fact be, I'll see the judge today about taking her away from Grandma."

Sarah doubled her fists at the threat, feeling hate for the man rising within her. Was it hate? She could not decide, but knew quite well there were no tender feelings for him. If he died somehow, she wouldn't shed a tear. Yet, the struggle within her stung terribly. How long could she continue to face up to this bully?

"Let's go, mister," the sheriff pulled the slaver toward the door. "The speech is over, you've had your say. You have nothing to do with where the girl lives."

Graybeard stomped out the door, never looking back.

"Goodbye, Running Fox." The sheriff tried to make it sound cheery.

"It's a house!" The Indian's face was rock hard.

"What?" The lawman turned sharply.

"This is a house. You called it a cabin."

"Oh, I know it's a house." The sheriff lowered his voice. "Sorry, didn't mean to insult you."

The men mounted up and rode east along the narrow lane leading to the main road. The Indian stood in the doorway and stared after them until they disappeared into the trees. With his back to the ladies, they didn't see the little half-smile crossing his lips.

The dark was ugly, and she hated the ugly. Yet, Sarah peered into the black hole, her young eyes searching for a glimpse of the runaway. "Mr. Jim, come on up. The men are gone."

Jim immediately stepped from the corner of the pit. The light struck his eyes and reflected to the girl. She breathed easy. As he climbed through the opening, before he even cleared the ladder, he whispered a big thanks to everyone. Within seconds he shoved the hearthstone into place.

The runaway shook like a leaf in a stiff breeze. "It be dark as the inside of a horse down there. That hole is sure enough the darkest place I ever saw – wouldn't want nuttin' any worst dark."

Chilled by the cool, damp hiding place, he walked near a window, and peeked out. Seeing no one, he moved a little closer and let the sun warm his face.

"The Good Book says bad folks is cast into the outer darkness. I be good – shore nuff. Dunt want to go to no place like that."

Everyone broke up in laughter, including Jim. He guffawed the loudest.

"Indian, that be some real quick thinkin', sending him to that hole. Never knowed ya had that hidin' place." Granny rubbed the back of her neck and shot him a quick side-glance. "There be one part of that there jawin' ya did with the sheriff that kinder bothered me a mite."

Running Fox peered down at the old lady, his brow wrinkled. He questioned her with his eyes, but he kept his mouth shut.

"I know what it is," Sarah spoke up. "It's . . ."

"Girl, don't be a buttin' in when ya ain't been talked to. I be a tellin' it. Now, uh, that part where ya told the sheriff there be no slave here. Was ya kinder, uh, strechin' the truth jist a little?"

Running Fox moved his eyes to where Sarah waited, her mouth open wide enough for a big fly to make a home. An uncomfortable silence filled the room. Granny and big Jim had decided to wait him out. The girl couldn't.

"Mama told me not to lie," Sarah finally spoke up. "'Just don't answer the slave catchers,' she told me."

The old Indian's eyes lit up. He smiled, and gave her a slight nod of agreement.

"Running Fox, ya stretched the truth purdy thin, don't ya think?"

"He done told the truth," Jim chimed in unexpectedly.

The old lady turned with a start. "How ya figurin' it, Jim?"

The runaway waited to see if the Indian would explain. Running Fox continued to play his game of silence. All the guesswork by Granny kept him silent.

"Miss Granny, there's a Quaker family I stayed with a few days ago. They told the marshals, there warn't no slave in the house."

"A Quaker said that? Why, I cain't hardly believe it."

"Miss Granny, this is what they's a thinkin.' This what they told me direct. They say, ol' Jim's no longer a slave. He's free. That's how they look at it. So, they's tellin' the truth. No slave here – no sir. I free, and I never goin' back. If they take me, it's because I be stone cold dead." Jim's voice quaked with emotion, and his body did the same. "No way I goin' alive!"

"I've heared that afore, Jim. Slave life be so bad, runaways would rather die tryin' to escape than live in bondage. Cain't say I'd be a thinkin' no different if I were in yer place. Guess ya told the truth, Indian." Granny closed one eye. "It might be a bit close to the edge though – don't ya think?"

Running Fox gave the slightest of smiles. "Close all right, mighty close."

10

Good News

"Little Miss, have ya ever made hay twists?"

"Yes ma'am, my mama taught me how."

"Good. It be gittin' cooler at night, and we be a needin' a fire soon. Got plenty of firewood, my patients supply me up with it, but I use the twists fer kindlin.'"

The girl gave a quizzical look. "It's summer!"

"I like to git an early start on the cold. Cain't be waitin' to the last minute."

Sarah gave a crooked, but knowing smile. She remembered Doctor Baum telling her that at times Granny was eccentric.

She wanted to understand the word, so she asked him what he meant. He told her the old lady does things her own way and many times quite differently from others. It wasn't wrong, just different.

"Sometimes our firewood wasn't much, so we put the twists on the fire to keep it going."

"Well, sounds like ya knowed all about it. I'm goin' to put ya in charge of makin' twists."

"I'll need to bring hay in from the shed." She started for the door. "I'm going right now!"

"Hold on there," Granny yelled. "Ya got other work first."

"Oh, no!" She jumped up and down. "I want to start now. It's gittin' cold soon, gotta git an early start." Sarah poked fun at the old lady, trying to imitate her.

Granny loved a good joke, and not to be outdone, she played along with the girl.

"Now Sarah girl, we gotta line things in order. Got some chores that go afore others. Ya knowed that, don't ya?"

"Yes, but having a fire is real important," she whined, working hard at keeping a straight face. "You said don't wait until the last minute; why, it could snow tonight!"

"Right ya be, and ya can start today, but . . ."

"I knew it," she cut her off and dashed for the door.

"Git back here."

"What now?" she huffed, a big frown sagged her lips.

Granny burst out laughing. "Sarah girl, I believe ya can keep right up with ol' Granny in tomfoolery."

The girl snickered softly, looking pleased.

"Work on it this afternoon," Granny went on, "we got dinner to fix. Cookin' up rabbit stew today. Doc's comin' by to eat with us. Look here, go git a few taters, five carrots and two big ol' onions from the cellar." The old lady handed her a small basket with a curved handle. "Load this up."

"How many potatoes?"

"Put yer thinkin' cap on, and ye decide. Ya look at the size of each tater and how much room the carrots and onions be a takin' up in the pot."

"All right, Granny."

Sarah stepped onto a little brick walkway leading to the cellar about twenty feet away. Granny had attached a rope onto the cellar door and strung it through a small wooden pulley to help Sarah with raising the door. Pulling on the rope, the door swung up, and Sarah leaned it against a post. Clutching her basket, she descended the steps into the cellar. Her fear of the dark lumped up in her throat, but with the sun shining brightly and the door facing the south, she had enough light to see. She relaxed a bit, and took five large carrots from a crock. Then, climbing onto a stool, the girl pulled down two large yellow onions hanging from the ceiling. A stalk of celery caught her eye. She stuck it in her basket and hurried up the cellar steps.

"Granny! I have the vegetables, ugh." She plopped the basket on the table. "I saw a stalk of celery and thought it might help the stew. Do you think it'll be good?"

"Now yer ol' noggin be used fer more than a hat rack. Good thinkin.' We'll put celery in the pot, too." She pulled it from the basket. "Did ya forget sompun?" She cocked her head, eyebrows raised.

"I know, you mean the potatoes. The basket didn't have enough space. I'm going now."

Sarah finished unloading the basket and then rushed back out the doorway. After deciding on four potatoes, she returned and placed the vegetables on the table.

As Granny cut the rabbit meat into small pieces, she asked Sarah to slice the carrots. After browning the meat in a skillet and preparing the other vegetables, the old lady placed everything into the pot. Sarah dropped her carrots in last.

"Put two pinches of salt in the pot." Granny pointed at the saltbox.

Sarah carefully reached inside the box and pinched the grains. Holding her hand over the pot she opened her fingers, and the salt dropped in. She did it again, rubbing her fingers together to remove all of the grains. Then Granny dropped two pinches of black pepper into the stew, also.

"I like pepper, but Mama didn't use it much, except for the . . ." Instinctively, the girl stopped.

"Except fer what?"

"Uh, let me smell it." She impulsively stuck her nose near the opening of the box.

"No! Don't git close . . ."

"Ah-choo! Ah-choo! Ah-choo! Ahhh-choooo!!" Sarah sneezed, and sneezed again. "I can't stop! Ah-choo! Ah-choo!" She bent over.

Grabbing the girl by the arm, Granny pulled Sarah against the washstand.

"Wash yer face, and the inside of yer nose," she yelled above the sneezing.

Sarah splashed water onto her face and into her nose. The sneezing finally stopped.

The old lady handed her a towel. "Dry yer face."

"What happened? I've never sneezed so much before."

"Girl, black pepper be strong, and when a little gits in yer nose it'll make ya sneeze. Ya sniffed a whole bucket load." She laughed, clapping her hands. "Ya almost stuck yer nose in it!"

"I only wanted to smell it. I like to smell spices and herbs."

"Shore, I like it, too. But, ya should ask about it first. I'd a told ya to go easy like. Guess ya stuck yer nose in where it didn't belong." Granny let out another big hee-haw. "Some people add salt to their food afore they ever taste it. What if it be salty already?"

"I guess they would ruin their food," Sarah reasoned.

"Ya guessed right. Don't be a thinkin' the food needs salt jist because it needed it last time. I be tryin' to tell ya sompun important. Check things first – ask questions. It be part of growing up." The old lady pulled herself up short, and softened her voice. "Ye'll learn."

Sarah nodded her head and thought back to the can of black pepper her mother kept hidden in the wood shed. *I forgot about it! Mama kept it to help the runaways.*

"What was ya sayin' about Rachel and the pepper?"

"Mama put pepper into the shoes of runaways. It confuses the slave catchers' dogs and they lose the scent of the slaves."

"Rachel was a smart one. Yer jist like her."

Sarah's face beamed like the sun on a cloudless day. *I love being exactly like her*, she thought.

"Got me a can of the stuff out in the drying shed. Use it on my packages, too." Granny winked.

Sarah chuckled, nodding her understanding.

Using a long handle wooden spoon, Granny stirred the pot, and clanked the lid down. "Girl, while the stew cooks let's go into the front room. Have ya ever made a rag rug?"

"No." Sarah shook her head.

"I want ya to make a rag rug and put it by yer bed." She gave the girl a hug. "Ya want to try it?"

"I sure do. In the winter my feet won't freeze." She shook like a duck shedding water. "May I take it with me when I leave to go live with my new parents?"

"Shore ya can. Ya can remember ol' Granny ever time ya put yer feet on it."

A frown crossed the girl's face. She had not thought of moving away from Granny and her friends at Wapakoneta. Unexpectedly a twinge of homesickness inched through her. She missed her farm. She missed helping her mother hide the slaves, too.

"I gotta pile of old rags and clothes over in the corner. Let's sort and cut the strips we'll use to make the rug. After we got all the strips cut, I'll show ya how to sew it together."

Forcing a smile with all the strength she could muster, the girl nodded her head.

Sarah tugged open the front door.

"Hello, Sarah," Doc greeted the girl. "How are you getting along? How's the arm?"

"I'm fine." She sat down alongside her work. "I'm making a rag rug to place by my bed, and Granny is helping me. We have a few more strips to cut, and then tomorrow we're going to sew it together."

"Good, after you learn how, make one for my office."

"Sure doctor, I'll make you a handsome one."

"What's cooking in the kitchen?" He sniffed. "It sure smells good."

"Come on, I'll show you!" She jumped to her feet and ran toward the kitchen door. "In here."

Strolling into the room, Doc took a deep breath. "Oh, Boy! I smell rabbit stew. Granny, how have you been?"

"Finer than frog fur. Come and sit."

Doc reached to lift the lid on the stew pot.

"Leave that pot be. I'll take care of servin' the grub. Now, git yer feet under the table."

Taking three bowls from the cupboard, Granny dipped the stew.

Sarah carefully placed the bowl in front of Doc. After all took a seat, the old lady invited Sarah to offer their thanks.

"Dear God, thank you for this rabbit stew. I hope Doctor Baum likes it. Please, send a good lady and man to become my parents. Tell Mama and my daddy I'm good most of the time. Amen."

"Girl, that was right nice." Granny winked.

"Thank you. I always remember to pray for my wish. Someday it will happen, I just know it.

"Doctor, do you want salt on your stew?" The mischievous girl peeked at Granny. *I'll test him*, she thought.

"I want to taste the stew first. Always taste it first." Doc took a bite. "Whoo-wee, it tastes exactly right. You made a delicious rabbit stew, Miss. Sarah. Remember now, always taste it first."

Sarah and Granny chuckled, quite amused.

"Everything tasted delicious, Granny." Doc leaned back in his chair, patting his stomach. "I'm about to pop."

The old lady pointed at Sarah. "Had a lotta help from my little girlfriend."

"She'll make a good wife someday," he bragged, reaching over and taking her hand.

Sarah's face turned red, and the doctor gave out a hearty laugh. Again he thanked them for the dinner and excused himself. He had patients to see.

After cleaning the dishes Sarah darted out the back door and headed straight to the hay shed. She grabbed an armload, and lugged it along the walk. Deciding to stay outside in the warm sunlight, she dropped the hay and sat next to her task. The girl liked the outdoors and had helped Granny several times in her herb garden near the back door. The old lady taught her various uses of herbs in fighting sickness, and Sarah learned how to use different herbs in preparing food, too. While soaking in the warmth she took handfuls of hay and twisted them tight. Her mother taught her twisted hay burned more slowly than a handful of hay thrown on the fire. After making several twists she entered the house and placed the little bundles alongside the fireplace.

While gazing at her work she turned her thoughts to her big wish. Every day Sarah imagined the joy of new parents. She daydreamed about her life as an orphan and how she hated it. She could not remember her daddy, and she so desperately wanted a family with a father and mother. They could never fully replace her mama – the girl knew that – but it would be a home. She loved Granny and staying with her, but she thought new parents might also have other children, and that would be better. She would love to have brothers and sisters.

I know Miss Mary has searched. Why does it take so long? I wonder where they live right now? When will they come to get me?

Granny walked through the doorway as Sarah began to pray.

"Dear Father," she prayed aloud, her voice thick with emotion. "I promise I'll be a good daughter. Please send my new parents soon. Oh, please, Lord. Amen."

The silence returned as she stared unseeing at the twists.

The old lady trembled; her eyes clouding with tears. She had heard the girl's low sobs at night, and knew Sarah hurt terribly. Granny prayed silently, *Lord, how will I ever let her go?* Slowly, quietly, she turned and left the room.

"Girl, how about playin' a game? An Indian game."

"I didn't know Indians played games."

"What ya think they did? Jist hunt, fish and shoot arrows at each other!" Granny howled with laughter.

Sarah giggled. "What's the game?"

"It be the straw game."

Granny pulled from the writing desk a handful of straws wrapped with a cord. The girl looked on with interest as the old lady placed the little square table from beside her rocker into the middle of the room.

"Sarah girl, this be how Running Fox tell'd me the tribes play the game. I got me two hundred straws in my hand, all the same length. Guess how many will be left after I divide them and count out one bunch by sixes."

"Huh?" Sarah gave a puzzled look.

"Let me showed ya how it works."

Holding the straws in her left hand, and with the thumb of her right, she divided the straws into two bunches. Granny laid aside one bunch of straws, and asked Sarah to guess a number between one and five. Then the old lady counted the straws six at a time and laid them down. Counting another six, she laid them down, and continued on until only less than six were left. The Indians called it the "remainder." Three straws remained, and Sarah had guessed two would remain. So, she missed by one on how many would be left.

"I understand." The girl pulled up a chair and set across from Granny. "How do we keep score to know who wins the game?"

"Each player gits a point if they guess right. That be where this little crock of apple seeds comes in." Granny pointed at the pottery she had placed on the table. "When ya git a point, ya git a seed from the crock. The person with the most seeds when we quit a playin' be the winner."

Sarah picked up the crock and looked inside. "Is it the way the Indians play the game?"

"Well, jist about. Depends on the tribe. Some guess the number afore they split the straws into two bunches, some don't. Others guess after, like we did. Several tribes bet on their games, we only play fer fun."

"What did they use to bet with?"

"They used animal pelts, beads, anything valuable to them."

Clapping her hands the girl cried out, "I love learning new things; let's play the game."

Sarah gathered the straws. Holding the two hundred straws in her left hand and dividing them, she asked Granny for a number.

The old lady squinted hard at the straw bunch. She scratched her head, rubbed her chin, and gave out a long hmmmmm, but finally settled on "four."

Sarah, not going through all the gyrations that Granny put herself through, guessed one. Counting out six straws at a time and laying them down, she held up the remaining five. They laughed, no winner. The game continued with each winning and losing, both having a happy time.

"Granny, I have two more seeds than you." The girl's eyes twinkled playfully. "Tell me when you're ready to give up."

"Look here girl, I ain't about to give in yet. Now . . ."

A rapid knock interrupted the old lady. Sarah raced to the door and opened it to a young, teenaged boy.

"Hello, Buford," she greeted him politely.

"Sarah."

Noticing the folded, single sheet of paper in the boy's hand, the girl pointed. "Is that a telegram? Do you still help at the telegraph office?"

"Yes, and this is addressed to Granny Evans. You ain't allowed to touch it."

Sarah gave the boy a puzzled look. She didn't care for him anyway, and his remark reminded her why. Buford always made fun of the girls at school, told half-true stories, and played jokes – sometimes mean ones – on the other children.

"I can take it and give it to Granny. I won't read it."

"No!" he said sharply. "Call Granny to the door."

"Buford boy, ol' Granny be right here." The woman moved in front of Sarah. "What ya jawin' about. Why cain't Sarah hand me a piece of paper?"

"It's addressed to you. I got orders – give it to Granny, nobody else. It's good news and you . . ."

"How ya knowed it be good news? Ya been readin' it?"

"No ma'am." The boy's attitude changed with the old lady at the door. "The telegraph operator told me. He read it, though!"

"Course, he read it, he wrote it down as it came off the wire."

The boy handed the telegram to Granny, turned on his heel, and ran away. She carefully unfolded the paper. Several seconds passed while she read and pondered on it. Finally, the corners of her mouth turned upward.

"Who's it from? What's the good news? Someone coming to visit? Did the stork come to your granddaughter's house? What . . ."

"Sarah Smith, take a breath!"

"Oops, sorry. What? Can I read it? What does it . . ."

"Girl, hobble yer lip!" Granny held up the telegram. "Looks like we be takin' a trip to Kentucky."

Sarah's forehead wrinkled, and her eyes narrowed. She did not speak.

"A family livin' on a farm close by Louisville wants ya to come visit. Mr. and Mrs. Stately be Christian folks and want a girl yer age to be their daughter. Looks like parents been found fer ya at last."

The girl felt her knees weaken, and two hundred straws scattered onto the floor. Words would not come. Her mind raced, and she felt many emotions course through her body. The day she had prayed about had arrived, but she greatly feared the jumble of feelings within her. Could it be her wish was about to come true? Time had come to take the first step by meeting these people, but she felt confused. Doubts unsettled her, and many questions flew through her mind.

"When?" she finally got in out. "When do we leave? Do I take all my things with me? Should I? No, maybe not, they might not want me. Granny, what should I do?" Sarah screeched.

The old lady cackled loudly, giving her a quick hug. "She found her talkin' box again."

II

Cincinnati

"What are those men doing in that field?" Sarah pressed her nose up tight against the window.

"Cain't rightly say," the old lady answered.

Everyone eyed the men as the cars began to slow to a stop at the station. Doctor Baum, Granny and Sarah had finally arrived in Cincinnati. From the Queen City the travelers would take a riverboat down the Ohio River to Louisville.

The Statelys lived near Louisville, and Sarah excitedly looked forward to the trip aboard the steamer. The hope of a new home, with parents she could love, blossomed within her heart. Yet, the thought of leaving Wapakoneta frightened her, and she tried her best to put the fear from her mind. She knew her wish would happen, and asked God to help her with the fear.

Forgetting her effort to act more grown up, she had shouted and jumped around Granny's front room when she learned the doctor would escort them on the trip. Ladies should always be escorted if at all possible. The doctor insisted they not travel alone.

"Sarah, I believe those men are playing the game of base ball." Squinting his eyes in thought, he tried to recall a memory. "I heard of it when I went through New York City, not long after my arrival from Germany. I believe they called one of the teams the Knickerbockers."

"Base ball." The girl whispered the words that really meant little to her. "What does that man do with the big stick he's holding?"

"He's called the 'striker,' and he tries to hit the ball when it's thrown. If he does, then he runs to the first base."

"What do the others do? When do they try to hit the ball? Or do they? Is there only one striker? What's the ball made out of? How do you know who wins. What are . . ."

"Let's go, girl!" Granny cut off the questions. "We gotta git one of them cabs to take us to the Burnett house. While we be fetchin' to the hotel, Doc can sort out the questions."

"But, Granny . . ."

"Come on! Let's git. After we settle in, we'll tramp on down to the levee, take a gander at these big city folks and git the lowdown on a steamer headin' to the Southland."

Without another word the three climbed into a large open carriage. The driver, a handsomely dressed black gentleman with graying hair slapped the reins. Sarah had never seen a Negro dressed so fine. She had only seen runaway slaves often arriving at the farm with worn and tattered clothing and the black stonecutter with his dusty soiled shirt and trousers. Sam and Eliza Smith did not dress that nice, even when they went to Sunday meeting. This trip would prove most exciting, a wonderful experience of learning, and Sarah drank it all in. What would be next? She could only wonder.

After checking in at the Burnett House and washing the road dust from their hands and faces, the ladies walked toward the river. Wearied by the long trip, Doc stayed behind and relaxed in the central courtyard of the hotel. Down on the streets the air was still damp from a morning fog that had settled over the river. Exciting scenes took place all around the girl and old lady. They missed nothing, taking it all in. All kinds of folks jammed the cobblestones. People of different colors, speaking strange languages, were seen and heard.

They continued strolling along Broadway Street, watching people. There were animals, too. Sarah loved the horses, and she saw several stray cats looking for a meal. A red-brown hound dog trotted across the street, appearing to be heading for the riverbank. Sarah sadly wondered if he was an orphan like her, another stray hoping for a home.

Several minutes later they neared the river. Getting her bearings, the girl realized they had reached the boatyards. An enormous jostling crowd excitedly chattered about a new steamboat launching. Sarah stared across the river, stunned to see the Kentucky side overrun with folks, also. In the middle of the river an anchored steamer awaited the splash down. The girl listened as men discussed the new boat. Each offered an opinion on how fast it would move through water.

Deciding to enter the conversation, Granny tapped one fellow on the shoulder. "What be goin' on here?"

"Guess you're from inland somewhere," the man replied, heckling her a bit.

"Been landlocked all my life. My pappy taked me on one of them pole boats when I was still wet behind the ears. Don't 'member it though, I warnt no bigger than a button when it happened."

The man pushed his way through the crowd. "Let's get a little closer, and I'll tell you about it."

Crowding ahead Sarah kept close to Granny. Their guide shouted he had with him a woman who had never seen a river before and wanted to see a boat. People close by laughed hard and granted the old lady room at the front.

I otter straighten him out. She chuckled, glancing sideways at Sarah. *Tell him this old gal has laid eyes on both, but I'm a thinkin' these folks already knowed it.*

"Madam, let me tell you how this whole thing is going to work." Their guide appeared quite pleased with "showing them the ropes." He knew much, could tell them much, and wasn't shy about doing it. "Cincinnati boasts several riverboat yards, and they launch these hulls one of two ways: end first or side first."

Noticing how it sat on the blocks, Sarah pointed. "This one is going in side first, isn't it?"

"Oh, you're a smart one." The guide seemed to mock her, and Granny gave him an evil-eye look. "Yes, it's going in sideways, and they've started removing the blocks and shores that hold it secure." Pointing, he sounded off, "Look at those lashings, soon they'll be the only things holding the boat."

The girl noticed large heavy timbers beneath the boat running down the riverbank to rivers edge.

Sarah pointed, "And those?"

"Those are the 'ways.' They are greased, so when the lashings are cut the hull will have a smooth ride to the water." He cut the air with his hand.

Distracting the ladies from the boat lecture, a brass band blared its music across the levee.

"This is quite a do-ins," Granny shouted over the music.

The man grinned and pointed at the riverboat. All of the blocks and shores had been removed, and men positioned themselves by the lashings. Each man held an ax.

Sarah pointed to movement on the boat deck. With a longing look the guide shouted, "Those people will ride it down the ways."

"Wheeeeee, I would love to do that," Sarah squealed.

The band stopped playing, and the electrifying silence gripped old and young alike. Gawking about, Granny noticed the people on board the hull were standing at the railing nearest the river. Flags and bunting hung from a rope stretched above their heads, and sunlight sparkled off fresh coats of white paint. Everyone looked in one direction, and the ladies followed. A man raised his hand.

"Ready!" he blared the command.

All of the men positioned themselves with axes raised.

"Cut lashings!"

As if by one force the axes sliced the air and slammed into the lashings. The leather snapped. A collective "ah" came from the crowd, and the boat slowly moved. A roar from the people aboard pierced the air as they picked up speed on the slide down the greased ways. A ride of a lifetime, and it ended with a huge splash and screams of delight from the crowd. The hull rolled and righted itself. Folks from the Kentucky side watched as a large wave moved toward them. It struck the riverbank, and people oohed and ahed.

The hull sat dead in the water, needing a tow to a spot below the boatyard. Here cabinetmakers would finish the deck and insides of the boat. It would have staterooms, dinning rooms, a kitchen, and cabins for the crew, plus the pilothouse. Once the workers completed those things, it would be towed upriver to a plant specializing in metal works. There, engines, boilers, and smokestacks would be installed. When completed, it would explore the rivers of America.

"Oh, Granny!" Sarah clapped her hands. "I barely believe my eyes."

"It's exciting every time I see a launching," their guide agreed, smiling big. "Lived here all my life, and I've seen several."

"Thanks fer givin' us the lowdown on it." Granny stuck out her hand to shake. "Where do I buy tickets fer passage on one of these here vessels?"

The man gestured toward the top of the levee, and the ladies were off to make their purchase. Since Doc stayed at the hotel, Granny had agreed to buy the tickets. Nearing the area where the boats were docked she noticed a newsstand offering newspapers from various places, including Cincinnati. As Sarah rested on a bench, the old lady turned the pages, glancing at the news and events. An announcement about the boat launching caught her eye. On the same page, two advertisements praised the merits of particular riverboats. The luxuries of the staterooms, beautiful carpet, superior wood paneling, plus the finest foods were described in language the old lady never used and barely understood. The riverboat *Golden Eagle* declared itself the last word in elegance. The *River Blade* claimed only a marvelous golden palace, fit for royalty, would truly describe its sophistication.

Whew! These here advertisements make ol' Granny want to put down stakes right in the middle of these things – permanent like, she laughed to herself. *I wonder if the* Golden Eagle *be a golden palace, too? Maybe the* River Blade *has kings strolling her decks.*

Granny laughed again, this time out loud.

Sitting in the hotel dinning room, Granny, Sarah and Doc awaited their supper. Hotel guests quickly filled the chairs around each table, everyone admiring the fine china and beautiful silverware.

Sarah fingered the gold edging of the plate. "Doctor Baum, we missed you at dinner."

"I drank coffee and tea at a little coffee house. Had soup, too. I sure enjoyed wandering around the shops – until I began longing for home." He frowned. "Guess I'm acting like a schoolboy."

"Look!" Sarah pointed at a large round table in the middle of the room set with a beautiful floral centerpiece. Eight table settings rested upon a beautiful white lace tablecloth. "A special guest must be with us tonight."

"I wonder if the president is visiting," Doc cracked. "What do you think, Sarah?"

"I don't know." Her voice took on a somber tone. "The only person I'm watching for is a slave catcher."

"A slave catcher? I don't understand." Doc scratched his beard.

"Mama told me slave catchers come to Cincinnati looking for runaways. It's not right! Ohio is a free state. They . . ."

"Young lady, I didn't know you knew about or even cared about runaway slaves. It's good of you to care. No one should be owned by another person." The doctor spat the words out as though they tasted bad to say them. "But, how would you know one if you saw him?"

"Ain't hard," Granny butted in. "Ya smell them afore ya see them."

Doc gave the old lady a confused look, not knowing what to say.

"Look!" Sarah called out again, pointing at the doorway.

All eyes turned as a strikingly distinguished looking fellow entered the room. Certainly not the president but dressed as finely. His presence immediately drew attention. A man at the next table announced, "It's Captain Fields!"

The doctor waved his hand at the fellow catching his attention. The man raised his eyebrows.

Doc whispered, "Who's this man?"

Quick came the reply, "James Fields, Captain of the *River Blade*."

"Ladies, this man is in charge of the steamer we will board tomorrow."

"The *River Blade*!" Sarah shrieked.

Those nearby giggled, and she felt herself blush. Doc chuckled.

The laughter caught the captain's attention as he neared the center table. Those with him took their seats, but Captain Fields moved on toward their table.

"There be no doubt about it," Granny cracked, "he be the biggest toad in the puddle."

"Oh, my," Sarah whispered, as her face pinked again. "He's coming this way!"

Doc's eyes twinkled in delight. He loved to tease the girl, and now was his opportunity. "You must be in trouble!" He gave her a worried look.

Sarah bowed her head. "Shhh," she whispered.

The captain arrived, and the doctor stood to greet him. About six feet tall and quite slim, James Fields sported neatly trimmed black whiskers that stretched well below his chin. He wore a fine suit with a diamond stickpin and carried a cherry wood cane.

"Good evening ladies," the captain bowed slightly. "I overheard the name of my fine vessel coming from this table."

"My name is John Baumgardner." Doc extended his hand.

"Mr. Baumgardner, pleased to meet you. I'm James Fields, captain of the *River Blade*."

"Captain, this is Granny Evans and Sarah Smith of Wapakoneta, Ohio."

"People in Wapak call him Doctor Baum," Sarah blurted.

"Pleased to meet all of you. Are you interested in the *River Blade*?"

"We are now," Sarah giggled. "Granny purchased tickets to travel on your ship."

Leaning back, the captain gave out a giant laugh. "It's no ship; it's a riverboat and the finest craft plying the yellow waters of the Ohio and the Mississippi, if I do say so myself. And, I do." He burst into laughter again.

"We be lookin' forward to plyin' with ya." Granny enjoyed the Captain's manner of speaking. He was a handsome man, too. The old lady had an eye for such things. At least she thought so.

"Thank you, ladies, you'll not be disappointed." The captain nodded at Doc. "So, you're a doctor?"

"Yes, I am.

"Doctor, will you be accompanying us on our trip to Louisville?"

"Yes, sir, I'm escorting the ladies."

"Good! I'm glad. I'm sure you'll enjoy it. Now if I can do anything for your comfort let me know. We certainly want to please our customers – say! We have many staterooms, and I can pull strings – get you what you want." The captain winked at the ladies.

Their faces beamed with amusement, enjoying the special attention.

"Thank you, Captain." Doc's face lit up with a thought. "Yes, I believe the ladies might enjoy the Ohio room."

"It's yours," Captain agreed laughing. "Ladies, I'll meet you at my boat tomorrow."

He bowed once more, turned, and strode to his table. Sarah glanced at Granny, and the old lady eyed the girl. Giggling, they looked at Doc.

"Looks as though the captain may have an eye for your attention, Granny," Doc cracked.

"Doc! I ain't interested in no man."

"Doctor Baum!" Sarah echoed. Her cheeks glowed red.

"Sir, your quail," the waiter addressed the doctor with a formal tone, placing a beautiful china plate before him. The roasted bird rested upon a bed of rice. The ladies were served lamb chops with roasted potatoes.

"Granny, after all of those years tending sheep," Doc caught her eye, "aren't you tired of lamb?"

"Naw, lamb chops be as good as it gets."

Sarah took a bite, chewing slowly, mouth closed like her mother taught her. "It's good! And the potatoes are good, too."

"These be mighty fancy fixin's all right. Might have to ask fer a second helpin.'"

The three ate their meals, fully enjoying every bite. Sarah quietly listened as folks at a nearby table described their harrowing ride down the Ohio from Pittsburgh. Her eyes bulged when hearing of the arrest of a wanted man. It happened right on the riverboat. The man had been caught transporting runaway slaves across the Ohio. Instantly, Sarah looked into Granny's eyes, staring for what seemed like minutes. The old lady returned the look, but neither uttered a word.

Doc finally interrupted the silence. "Ladies, the *River Blade* casts off at noon tomorrow. We will have all morning to gather our things. If we prepare ourselves early enough I want to stop by a little coffeehouse I found. Another delicious cup of African Java would be wonderful. I believe you might enjoy it," he assured them. "They have many varieties of tea, also."

Sarah closed her eyes, thinking of happy times at the farm. "I love tea." She turned to Doc. "Sometimes Mama and I would drink it in the evenings as we sat before the fire. Those were happy times. I hope my new parents do things like Mama. Oh! Granny, my wish – my prayer – is for a new mother, like Mama."

"Little Miss, ya keep a prayin' about it, God will take care of ya."

Granny's faith held strong, and Sarah believed in the old lady, but even more in her Lord.

"We be early risers, look forward to a cup of the grind."

"Doctor Baum, may I have a sarsaparilla? I love the taste."

Grinning big, Doc answered, "Sure, and I'll buy you a stick of candy, too."

After they finished their meals the waiter returned immediately to remove the plates.

"Mister, them there chops reminded me of home. The feller that cooked them must be from Northeast Ohio." The old lady gave her tummy a quick pat. "I be as full as a tick on a big dog."

"The quail tasted wonderful," Doc agreed, clapping his hands. "Tell the chef it made my day."

The ladies smiled and nodded their agreement.

12

The Levee

The carriage wheeled to a stop on the landing near the *River Blade*. The driver set the bags and trunks on the ground as Doc and the ladies stepped from the cab. Activity swirled around them, and of course, they tried to take it all in. Finding it impossible, the group still enjoyed trying. The steamboat sat with its stage down and several roustabouts worked quickly to bring cargo aboard.

"Did I tell you the truth last night?" Doc asked. "That coffee house has wonderful drinks."

"I love sarsaparilla." Sarah's dimples quivered as she licked her lips. "Thank you, and thank you for the peppermint stick."

"Ya didn't lie," Granny hooted. "Hope this here boat has some of that African Jafer. It'll beat the swill that restaurant in Wapak calls coffee."

"Java, Granny. It's called African Java," Sarah told her politely but felt somewhat uneasy correcting the old lady.

"African Jafer, that be close. I jist got a bit of a twisted accent on it."

Sarah sighed, mostly inside. The girl knew changing Granny's talk wasn't going to happen. She returned to watching the *River Blade* being loaded.

Captain Field's riverboat navigated the waters from Cincinnati to New Orleans. After leaving Louisville it would make several stops, one at Cairo, Illinois. At that riverboat town, many of the passengers would disembark and board other steamers traveling north on the

Mississippi River to St. Louis. From there they would paddlewheel up the Missouri River for destinations in the Dakota Territory.

Several steamboats were nosed into the shore, each in various stages of loading or unloading passengers and cargo. Sitting beside the *River Blade*, the *Golden Eagle* took on crates of pork. Several landings along the Ohio north to Pittsburgh would receive its freight.

A sternwheeler alongside the *Golden Eagle* sounded a large sliver bell, and the band aboard struck up a tune. A few stragglers hurried up the stage. Sarah pointed. Three giant smoke stacks poured black smoke as the firemen increased the fuel in the fireboxes.

"It won't be long now," Doc told them. "They're getting up a head of steam!"

Sarah's eyes danced with excitement. "I can hardly wait until we leave." As the bell once more tolled and the band played on, the girl, almost screaming it, exclaimed, "It's quite exciting!"

The sound of distant thunder could be heard, and Granny cocked an ear to listen.

"Sounds like them taters be a rollin' up yonder." Pointing toward Heaven, she looked for clouds on a sunny day.

A man passing along laughed at the comment. "That isn't the forecast of rain, it's the riverboat."

The bells rang and the paddle wheel slowly turned, churning the yellow water. The steamboat backed into the middle of the river.

The gentleman remarked over his shoulder, "The thunder you hear is steam." He gave them a slight wave and disappeared into the crowd.

"Greetings folks! You're welcome to board the *River Blade* anytime," Captain Fields offered. "I'll have your things taken aboard immediately."

"Thank you, Captain." Doc extended his hand to shake. "We are taking pleasure in watching the crowd and boats. I've seen a number of real characters around here. Looks to me as though Cincinnati draws folks from all parts of the world."

Moving his hand through the air Captain Fields pointed. "Yes, sir! They come from all over. You'll see white, black, redskins, yellow people from the Orient. All kinds here."

"All kinds of clothin', too," Granny interjected. "Strange lookin' garb."

"Ha! I imagine in their country they say the same about your hoop-skirts and poke bonnets."

Everyone joined the laughter.

"I must attend to my boat," he went on, "but look forward to seeing you aboard. Oh, by the by ladies, I have written your names beside the Ohio room on my list."

Baaa, baa, baa. Hearing the familiar sound the old lady whirled about and looked toward the ridge of the levee. A small flock of sheep milled about.

"I knowed that sound! Used a hatchel many a time."

The flock refused to descend the slope, appearing spooked by the noisy paddleboats belching smoke and steam. The shepherds struggled to restrain them from scattering.

"I wonder if one of the boats is taking them on," Sarah asked.

"Shore could be. Horses boarded the *River Blade* a whiles back, and I sawed chicken coops filled with roosters hauled on, too."

"It'll be a big chore moving those sheep even close to the boats, let alone get them aboard," Sarah laughed her words. "Maybe those big roustabouts will pick them up and carry them on."

"Wouldn't want to try it," Granny came back. "Sheep will bite ya knowed."

"No," Sarah's eyes grew big, "I've never heard that before."

Granny pointed at the flock moving about on the ridge. "Captain Fields, answer me sompun."

"By all means," he declared loudly, chuckling at their discussion. "I aim to please my passengers."

"Them sheep, they gonna be hauled on one of the boats?"

"Yes, Ma'am, that they are," he answered happily. "The *River Blade* is transporting them to a buyer in Louisville."

"My husband and me kept sheep fer years, and I've a likin' fer them, but gittin' them aboard that there boat – well, I cain't see it a happenin.' Them critters cain't be herded like cattle."

"We know all about sheep. Taken them aboard before, but you're right, they can't be herded. Doesn't matter though, we have Fred."

"Fred?" Granny wrinkled her nose in thought.

"Sure, Fred will have them aboard in no time." His mysterious eyes twinkled. "He'll be along shortly – you remain here and watch. I must hurry, the first bell tolls soon. It's almost eleven o'clock. See you folks aboard the *River Blade*."

"Thank you for the Ohio room." Sarah gave a quick point to the steamboat.

He tipped his cap and strolled away, disappearing into the hundreds of people milling about the cobblestone levee.

Granny pointed a bony finger to the ridge. "Let's be gittin' further up the levee. I want to git a clear view of this here Fred feller."

As the three closed the distance between them and the bleating animals, one of the shepherds cried out, pointing toward the river's edge. "Fred!"

All eyes turned as one to catch a peek at the man who wielded such control over these nervous wooly beasts. Granny peered down the pavement of cobblestones, straining to see. See what? Well – she wasn't sure.

"Ya lay eyes on the feller, yet?"

"No."

"Not, yet," Sarah added.

They kept a close eye to the crowd, trying to catch a glimpse of this pied piper. They only saw hundreds of people going about their business and one billy goat on the loose.

"Hmmmmm," Granny sighed, watching the smug goat sashay along the levee. *Can a goat be smug?* She jested to herself. *Hmmmmm, this here billy goat ain't a runnin' loose. Naw – there be no way. Cain't be no way. Fred!*

"Folks, I'm a thinkin' – we be a lookin' at Fred!" She pointed at the short horned, white goateed animal.

Standing on tiptoes, Sarah asked, "Where?"

"Right there." The girl followed Granny's finger as it pointed straight at the goat strutting within ten feet of the group.

"The goat?" Doc pointed, too.

"That goat?" Sarah echoed.

"I should have knowed! Sheep will foller a goat or ram. Seen it happen."

Fred acted as though he did not even notice the sheep. The shepherds stood still and watched the billy goat slowly enter the flock. He disappeared.

Granny peeked at Sarah with a scrunched face, one eye shut. "Watch the flock. I've never laid eyes on a trained goat afore, but I guess I be lookin' at one now."

The three scanned the flock as the sheep continued to mill about. All of a sudden Fred reappeared. Taking the same pathway down the landing, he marched between crates of cargo and bales of cotton. The lambs meekly followed in apple pie order. At the river's edge they moved up the stage and into the pen on the boiler deck.

"Now, if that pert near don't pluck the feathers off a chicken." The old lady howled loudly. "Beats all I've ever sawed."

Sarah hugged Granny's neck so hard and long the old lady yelped for air. "This trip will have lots of new things. It's so exciting!"

"It be excitin' all right! Better yet, fer shore, if I can do a little breathin' from time to time."

Clang, clang, clang. The big silver bell atop the *River Blade* tolled its welcome. Pulling the colorful rope attached to the bell, Captain James Fields stood beside the pilothouse waving at the boarding passengers.

Granny pulled a small silver pocket watch from her knitting bag. "One hour afore we leave. Look at that there wharf. There be fifteen boats tied up. All of this cargo is either waitin' to load, or its jist got here and gonna be delivered to shops and factories all over. There jist could be sompun here goin' to Wapak."

"Granny, I saw a crate marked 'Dayton.'" Sarah pointed to several large wooden boxes stacked three and four high.

Tilting her head in the direction of a riverboat disembarking its passengers, Granny snapped, "Now there's a sight!"

Several brightly painted wagons rolled onto the cobblestone pavement of the levee.

"They're swarming everywhere," she complained, moving her hand in a semi-circle.

Dressed in bright, multicolored clothes, one hundred men, women and children scattered among the travelers arriving and departing the riverboats. Their wagons gathered together, with one or two barking dogs hanging out of each vehicle.

"Gypsies!" Granny gasped. "Hold on to everythin' not tied down. I've seen the likes of them afore. They come regular through the Western Reserve years ago." She pulled her knitting bag tight under her arm. "Keep a eyeball on yer handbag."

"Why?" Sarah asked. "They really look like friendly, happy people."

"Shore, they be friendly all right, but watch them." Granny had a cranky tone. "Years ago they camped on our property, staking out their tents and their fice dogs. The loud music, along with the barking animals, frightened our sheep. When they finally moved on, we were on the little end of the horn when we counted our flocks – every time!"

The colorful, animated folks reached the three quickly.

"Ma'am, I can tell your future," the lady addressed Granny. "For a tiny price indeed you will know what awaits you in the days to come." Her painted red lips smiled big, teeth showing.

Granny studied her face and general appearance. She wore several necklaces made of many colored beads. A gold bracelet adorned her left wrist and round gold rings were attached to her ear lobes. She wore a dress of many colors with a red sash tied at the waist. Along with her painted red lips, her cheeks were lightly smeared with the same crimson.

"If I were a lookin' fer a fortune teller I would call on ya," Granny talked back, giving it her best to be nice, "but I be on a trip, and I cain't see gittin' it ruined by knowin' what be gonna happen."

Behind her, Granny's companions smiled and nodded, hoping the Gypsies would move along.

"I have pretty things, Miss." Sarah felt a tug on her dress. Looking over she saw a little girl of about seven holding several beaded necklaces. Dressed brightly, she too wore gold earrings.

"Ma'am," the lady persisted with Granny, "I would never ruin your trip. I will only tell you happy things in your future."

"I have lots of pretty scarves," the little girl raised her arm showing Sarah the colorful cloth loosely tied to her forearm.

"That be a problem, Miss," Granny told the woman.

"Take a scarf, see what you think," the little Gypsy persisted. "Ma'am, try one on your head."

"Ooooooh," Sarah exclaimed, dazzled by the pretty silks.

"Ma'am, how can I possibly hurt you?" The lady batted her eyelashes. "It is good to know what will happen in the days to come." She quickly grasped the old lady's hand. "You can change it if you don't like it."

"These pretty beads – they will look beautiful around your neck," the little girl went on, imitating her partner.

The Gypsy girls seemed harmless enough, and Doc stepped backward watching with amusement as they chattered away. If it had been Gypsy men he would have told them to move on.

Sarah touched one of the scarves moving it between her fingers.

A mistake, Doc told himself.

Granny pulled her hand back slightly with the Gypsy still attached.

With a pretty face and a devilish smile, the little Gypsy teased, "Put the scarf on, you will look sooo pretty!"

"I only need to see the palm of your hand," the older girl kept on.

"I'll untie it so you may try it on," the little one pestered Sarah.

Continuing to yap, the Gypsy once more pulled Granny's hand toward herself, pleading, "Only a quick peek," she insisted, smiling ever so sweetly.

"Now, lookee here, Miss, I ain't interested." Granny's firm manner would have put off most folks, but not these two. The gypsies had been this way before. They would not be discouraged so easily.

Placing her beads on the cobblestones the little girl removed the beautiful scarf.

"Oh, Madam," the woman cried out as she turned Granny's hand over and studied her palm.

With her smile fading fast, Granny barked, "Now, Miss, I don't need to knowed my future."

Handing the colorful scarf to Sarah, the little girl cheerfully squeaked in a mouse – like voice, "Put this around your head, pretty girl."

The lady began her speech to Granny. "I see wonderful things coming to you. Oh, I know you will want to hear all about them. For a small coin I will unfold these beautiful events."

"You are so pretty!" the little girl tried batting her eyes lashes, mimicking the older. "Yes, this is for you. It is meant only for your head."

"Lady, I don't want to knowed nuttin ahead of time." Granny closed her hand, yanking it away. "Don't ya be a tryin' to cut shines with me."

Sarah reached into her handbag for the coins. "I like it."

Rachel would have told her not to waste her money. Doc smiled.

"Ma'am," the young lady smiled, refusing to quit. "We have items on our wagon you'll be interested in. Now if you'll step this way my uncles can show you . . ."

Clang, clang, the big bell on the *River Blade* tolled the warning.

"Ain't interested!" Granny turned to walk away. "Our boat's a pullin' out in half an hour. We gotta go."

The small girl whimpered, sad eyed. "You want a scarf, too, like the little one?" She pointed at Sarah.

"No!" Granny barked. "We gotta high tail it." Grabbing Sarah by the arm, she gently tugged.

Both gypsies continued to call after them, "We have other items."

Granny kept her head up and eyes straight ahead. "Keep a walkin', don't look back."

Sarah giggled, thinking the old lady took it much too seriously.

Spying a big roustabout carrying a large keg, Doc scooted alongside, walking in step with the man. Hiding from the two Gypsy girls, he made his escape and caught up with the ladies. Passing row after row of barrels filled with pork, flour, dried fruit, hams, bacon, cane sugar, salt, and molasses, they made their way toward the riverboat. The variety of items shipped on the boats surprised everyone. Stacks of lumber, crates of soap, boxes of candles, and sacks of coffee beans blanketed the landing. Lake and river ice from the far North, covered with insulating sawdust and wrapped with tarps, awaited shipment south. In another area sat railroad iron for loading to points unknown. Nearing the *River Blade*, Granny paused and watched a buggy pushed aboard, followed by a two-seat carriage. She pointed at the deck where several horses, coops of chickens, and the sheep noisily made their presence known. A man passed by pulling a small cart full of mail that had been wheeled off one of the Louisville boats.

"Granny!" Sarah pointed an excited shaky finger at a nearby paddle wheeler.

Accompanied by their handlers, an elephant, and several beautiful horses, along with other strange animals, unloaded onto the levee. A man drew attention to the circus with his juggling act.

"I want to see the circus," Sarah shrieked.

"Sorry, but it be time to git." Granny hurried onto the boarding stage and waved at Sarah. "Girl, fetch yourself over here, and be quick about it."

The big silver bell tolled its last warning. Quickly, Sarah scurried aboard. She knew it would not be long until she met her new parents.

13

Mrs. Stately

Sarah's ringlets bounced as the carriage moved along the muddy road. Pointing to a lush green meadow surrounded by a white rail fence, Sarah squealed with delight at three chestnut colored horses dashing through the wild flowers. The Ohio River could still be seen in the distance as the carriage turned onto the long drive leading to the Stately home.

The Statelys were Christians and well known in Jefferson County. The telegram Granny received from her cousin, advised he did not know them personally but others recommended them.

Sarah sat up front with the carriage driver. "Where's the house?"

He motioned toward the woods ahead. "Through the trees, Miss."

Freshly whitewashed rail fences corralled several fine looking horses. They lazily grazed among the pretty, many colored wildflowers that dotted the meadows.

"Do the Statelys own all of these horses and fields?"

"Yes, ma'am."

"Oh, my!"

The telegram revealed little, only that the Statelys lived on a farm and did not have children. Sarah's farm in Auglaize County did not come close to comparing with this place.

"Their house sits in a meadow on the other side of the little woods."

The girl shifted uncomfortably in her seat. "How do you know about the Statelys?"

The carriage entered the shade of the thin strip of trees.

"Occasionally, I bring men out here to conduct business."

Granny suddenly had an uneasy twinge run through her. "What be their business?"

The carriage emerged from the woods. "We're here. This is the Stately home." The question remained unanswered.

The carriage turned onto a circle driveway and stopped in front of the largest house Sarah had ever laid eyes on. Gleaming with white paint, several large round columns supported the second story. The girl slowly turned her head toward Granny, and her mouth dropped open, wide enough for a big horned cow to walk in.

"Somebody lives here?" she gasped.

The driver chuckled. "The Statelys do."

A young black man opened the door of the carriage. Standing aside, he waited as the riders stepped out.

"Looks to be these folks have enough money to burn a wet dog," Granny teased. "Guess they be the big bugs in this here neck of the woods."

"That's understating it," agreed the doctor.

"I can't live here! This isn't a house. It's . . . I don't know what." She gazed up at the second story balconies. "This isn't a house."

"Sarah, we came a long way to meet these folks," Doc pointed out. "Don't decide by the first look. Give them a chance."

"Shore, ya might catch a likin' to it," Granny added, laying a gentle hand on her shoulder.

The girl's frown deepened, but she kept her thoughts to herself. The group strolled along the red brick that led to the front door. At the same time the carriage moved around the circle drive and disappeared through the trees. The driver had agreed to return tomorrow.

Sarah raised the huge doorknocker, slamming it three times.

"They otter heared that." Granny gave out a big hee-haw.

Within seconds the giant door opened, and a tall black man smiled at them. Dressed in a tailored black suit with a snow-white shirt, his sliver hair and lined face revealed he had been living many years.

"My name be Granny Evans, and this here be Sarah Smith and Doctor John Baumgardner. Come to see Mr. and Mrs. Stately."

"Please, folks, come in," the old gentleman invited.

He stood aside, and the travelers walked into a large hall. Golden wallpaper, bordered in silver, covered the walls. A large painting of a man hung above a sideboard, and fresh flowers filled a large gold and white vase that adorned the giant piece of furniture.

The man led the visitors into a parlor where he offered them a chair. After announcing Mrs. Stately would be with them shortly, the butler closed the door. The three looked at each other and then timidly glanced around the room. Bookcases lined three walls, and a large chandelier hung from the high ceiling. A stone fireplace filled the entire fourth wall, with a fierce looking animal staring at them from above the mantle. Granny and Doc settled into deep leather chairs while Sarah walked about looking things over.

The girl shook her head in disbelief. "I thought my daddy had a lot of books." Picking up a magazine from the lamp table beside Granny, she read, "*Millennial Harbinger*. Granny, this is Mr. Campbell's paper! Mama reads it all the time. Maybe Mrs. Stately is like Mama."

"Hope so, little one."

The old lady looked Sarah up and down with an approving glint in her eye. She liked the girl's red dress, neatly trimmed with white lace.

"Ya look neat as a rooster wearin' stockins," Granny jested. "Shore beats them tow shirts ya use to wear as a little tyke. These folks cain't help but want ya. No doubt about it."

The door opened, a woman in her late thirties entered and crossed the room. She wore a beautiful sky blue dress, and her dark brown hair sat in a bun. The girl's eyes fixed on one of the prettiest ladies she had ever seen. The woman gave Sarah a warm smile. Granny and Doc rose from their chairs to greet her.

"Hello, I am Mrs. Stately." The woman gave Granny a slightly quizzical look, and quickly focused on Doc. The old lady noticed it but passed it off.

"The name be Granny Evans, and this here be Doctor John Baumgardner. The little one, Sarah Smith."

I'm not a little one, Sarah thought to herself. *I wish Granny would stop saying that.*

"Pleased to meet you, Mrs. Stately." Doc nodded.

She returned the nod, saying nothing.

"Hello, Ma'am," Sarah greeted with a cheery voice.

The lady briefly looked Sarah's way and then back to Doc. Mrs. Stately assumed more than she should, including the notion Dr. Baum was Sarah's guardian. "So, Sarah is the poor little orphan girl."

"I'm not poor," Sarah blurted out. "I am an orphan though."

She turned toward the girl. "What kind of work did your father do?"

"He preached the Gospel and farmed, too." The girl beamed with pride. "My mama helped him."

"All preachers are as poor as Job's turkey, except Alexander Campbell." She pointed to his periodical on the table. "He inherited most of his wealth from his father-in-law."

Sarah's face crumbled like soft shale, she bit her lower lip. Granny gave the girl a side-glance and saw the hurt in her eyes. Whether she intended it or not, Mrs. Stately's remark hurt Sarah deeply.

"Look here," the old lady spoke up, "the Smiths weren't poor. The girl's granddaddy had a large plantation in Virginia. The Smith's weren't a hurtin' none." Granny's voice had turned ice cold, and she blew the frost Mrs. Stately's way. "What's all this got to do with Sarah?"

"Of course, Miss-uh?"

"Evans!" Granny reminded her.

"Yes, Miss Evans. Sarah's lack of money has nothing to do with her acceptance into the Stately home. We will talk further in the flower garden." Though it appeared her smile was forced, it returned, and she gave it to Sarah. The girl nodded, her lips a thin straight line.

The woman picked up a little bell from the table and rang it. Immediately, the door opened and a teenaged black girl, wearing a black dress with a white apron, entered the room.

"Susie, bring tea and cakes to the garden." The command was sharp.

"Yes, Ma'am." The black girl curtsied, whirled about and dashed away.

"Please, follow me." She had said please, but it sounded more like an order.

The garden area at the back of the house overflowed with several kinds of flowers. Various bushes along the walkways burst with color, and heavy vines intertwined lattice arbors. Rose fragrance floated through the air.

Sitting in chairs overlooking the flower garden, the four had a beautiful view of a wooded area. It stood about a quarter-mile away, and a narrow lane faded into it.

Pointing, Granny asked, "Where does that slantindicular road go?"

"The fields are on the other side. It is where our crops are planted."

"Is Mr. Stately here?" the girl asked. "Will I meet him today? Does he work with the horses I saw?"

"He will be here at suppertime. He is buying, uh – conducting business in Louisville."

A black man tended roses in the garden. Sarah noticed he appeared much older than the man who answered the door. "Who's that man?"

Mrs. Stately gave a strained chuckle. "You are full of questions, aren't you, little girl? It does not matter who he is, does it?"

"Yes," came the nervous reply. *Now Mrs. Stately is calling me little girl.*

Whew! Granny thought to herself. *This woman be as cold as a big carp in a frozen creek.*

"If you must know, he is the gardener. He keeps the flowers and plants looking pretty."

"He's good at it!"

Ignoring the remark, Mrs. Stately stared at Doc. "We are Christians, and we want a good Christian girl." Her voice still carried the cool tone. "We have not been blessed with children, so we will take second best if we must. A good Christian orphan will do, but she must be well-mannered and obedient."

Granny and Sarah gawked at each other. Doc rubbed his beard thinking of what to say.

"Sarah is a mighty fine young lady. Her daddy preached the Good Book, and her mother, a wonderful Christian lady, lived it. They . . ."

"Doctor, that may be all well and good, but I am talking about the girl." The woman spoke the words in an even manner, but with a big artificial smile. "We do not want to take on any problem child. She must be well behaved and in good health. Mr. Stately and I have enough problems worrying about our farm and the crop prices. Plus, there's the daily worry of keeping the workers from stealing us into poverty. On top of all that, there is talk of war."

"Mrs. Stately," Doc began, "I . . ."

"Where is that girl?" she snapped. "Those cakes and tea should have been served by now. Excuse me."

Rushing away, the lady disappeared through the back doors. Granny, Doc and Sarah stared at each other, not believing what they had seen and heard.

Getting to her feet, Sarah walked into the garden. Seeing a butterfly, she stopped to watch the lovely creature take nectar from a flower. The colorful wings of orange, dotted with black circles, fluttered softly. The girl moved closer. Into the flower went the small tube from the butterfly's head. Sucking the nectar, the feathery creature spread its wings and revealed the amazing handiwork of one of God's most beautiful creations. It flitted away.

Hearing the gardener close by, Sarah turned her head. He smiled faintly. With eyes warm and friendly he gave her a little wink and a slight wave of the hand.

"Hello," Sarah called.

"Miss." He dipped his head toward her in greeting.

"This flower garden is beautiful. Mrs. Stately said you take care of it."

"That's so."

"I saw a butterfly on the flowers. It kept sticking something into the middle of each one."

"It eats that way. Guess it's like a little straw. It curls against the face when it ain't a feedin.'"

"I love butterflies." A smile took up her whole face. "They don't

107

seem to have any troubles. They can fly wherever they want to go. Maybe even to Heaven."

"They's free for shore." Glancing toward the house and around the garden, he lowered his voice. "I shore like to knows how they feel. Bet they can fly across the Ohio."

Sarah stared back with questioning eyes. *This man isn't happy. He talks like the runaways Mama helps, but he can't be a slave. Mr. and Mrs. Stately are Christians. They wouldn't keep slaves.* "Butterflies are so little." She held her thumb and forefinger close together. "I don't think they can fly across a river."

"How they git to Heaven then? That be a ways."

Thinking hard about it, Sarah nodded in agreement. "You're right, they can fly across the river, all the way to Ohio." She paused, wondering if she should continue. Yes, she decided to hint. "Maybe even farther – all the way to Canada."

His eyes lit up, and his head, crowned with a handsome crop of sliver hair, bobbed ever so slightly. The girl wrinkled her brow, knowingly. Once again she paused, thinking what to say next.

Then, suddenly, as though shot with a pistol, the old man collapsed between two rose bushes. Immediately, Sarah scurried to his side. *Oh, my! He looks poorly.*

"Miss," his voice now weak, "things like butterflies, and people like me . . . can . . . can do lots a things folks don't knows we can." The twinkle in his eyes had faded, and his eyelids began to close. "I . . ." His voice trailed off into silence. He tried again to continue, he could not. Toppling sideways, he lay still.

"Sir!" Sarah cried out. "Mister!"

The old man remained quiet. For Sarah though, living through that terrible day of screams and shouts, when Blackie raced out of control into the meadow, that snake on the road day, that day had just begun again. The sight of her mother lying under the buggy, as this old man lay deathly quiet in front of her now, flashed through Sarah's mind. It shot cold chills down her spine, all the way to her toes. She trembled as never before, and everyone felt the screams.

"Doctor Baum! Granny! Doctor, please!"

Doc and Granny sprung from their chairs and rushed toward the heart-gripping shrieks. Kneeling beside the gardener, Doc gently placed his fingers on the man's neck.

"His pulse is weak. Let's get him into the shade and be quick about it."

"What is happening?" Mrs. Stately irritably shouted from the back porch.

"Your gardener – he's ill," Doc replied.

"Take the bucket of water by the gate, give him a drink." Her tone sounded almost uncaring. "He will be all right."

"We must put him into the shade, immediately! Please call for help," Doc insisted.

Not accustomed to taking orders, Mrs. Stately's jaw tightened and her lips turned white. Putting her hands to her hips, she stared hard at the doctor. Doc locked onto her gaze and returned the stare.

Granny's face flushed an angry red as she got to her feet and made a beeline for the woman. Pointing a finger backwards at the gardener as she charged straight ahead, the old lady showed she could give orders, too. "This here feller be in a bad way; fetch some help out here, and do it now!"

Snatching a bell from the table, Mrs. Stately shook it furiously. The man, who answered the door, two teenaged girls wearing white aprons over black dresses, and another lady about the age of Mrs. Stately, with flour on her face, answered the bell. All were Negroes.

Waving them over, she barked out the command, "Charlie is out there on the ground, help get him to the shade."

Immediately all four hurried to the spot where the gardener had fallen. With Doc's help they carried him into the shade of a large oak. Granny began to cool him with a cloth soaked in cold well water. Again the angry bell sounded and the four helpers rushed to Mrs. Stately. Glancing over at Granny, Doc mumbled something to her about the "bell ringer." She smirked her agreement.

Sarah knelt beside Charlie and took his hand. "Don't die, Mr. Charlie," she whispered tearfully. "You must be a butterfly – you must."

Granny shrugged her shoulders at the remark and continued to cool his head. She wondered though, what did Sarah mean? By the girl's tone, it certainly wasn't a schoolyard game. The sound of hooves and the creak of a donkey cart interrupted her thoughts. The teenager who went for the tea and cakes now pulled up alongside the group.

Without a flicker of emotion, she spoke the words. "Mistis says take him to the hut."

Doc stood up. "The hut? What hut?"

"The hut where he sleeps."

They placed old Charlie on the hay, and Doc climbed aboard.

"The Mistis won't like it." Susie shook her head. "I'll git help when I git to the hut."

Showing his German stubbornness, Doc replied, "He's my patient now; I'll go with him."

"You's the white man, I do what ya says." She slapped the reins, and the cart moved with a jerk. The donkey slowly plodded down a narrow wagon path that finally disappeared into the green.

Granny and Sarah returned to the back porch where Mrs. Stately impatiently waited. A peaceful quiet followed as the three sipped tea. Lost in their own thoughts, the cakes remained untouched.

Mrs. Stately considered whether having the girl visit might not have been a good idea. Granny's thoughts were much the same.

Sarah kept her eyes on the spot where the donkey cart vanished into the trees. She thought about Charlie. She recalled how much she wanted to take care of Polly and Joseph, not let them starve. Now, it was this gardener. She must talk to him again. The steel woven into her frame would not let her give up, at least not without a fight. Why she cared so much was anybody's guess, but she knew her feelings and she would not be satisfied until she did everything possible to help the old gentleman. If he wanted across the River, somehow she would see him across. She trusted God for what she couldn't do on her own.

While Sarah did her figuring, Granny eyed the girl, and then took a look at Mrs. Stately. Studying their faces, she wondered to herself. *Sompun ain't right about this here place. Don't think Eli and Rachel would be a likin' what happened here today. What be the Mister like? Wonder if he be as high-falutin' as her.*

"Why ya want Sarah?"

Mrs. Stately's mean little eyes twitched slightly, and they opened a crack wider. She slowly turned her head. "What did you say, Miss Evans? I was paying you no mind."

"Why ya want Sarah?" Granny didn't hide her feelings. "You want a daughter, or maybe a servant girl?"

The girl's eyes widened as she glanced from woman to woman. *Granny's voice is too gruff.*

"Miss Evans, if you must know, I am quite anxious to have a daughter. I have servants," she snapped, her voice cold as the arctic. "This is really none of your affair. My business is with the doctor. I prefer to speak with him concerning the child. He is her guardian, isn't he?"

"He ain't here, and he ain't her guardian, no way. I am. The judge appointed me her guardian after the death of her mother. Her mother's good friend be too sickly to take on anymore children." *Well, this be a real kick in the teeth,* Granny told herself. *This woman thinks I be some seven by nine chucklehead.* "Ya gonna have to talk with me."

Leaning forward, Sarah asked politely, "What happened to your children, Mrs. Stately?"

"We were never blessed with children."

Taking a bite of the little cake, Sarah's eyes twinkled with delight. "Mmmmmm, this is good. I've never had a cake like this. What's in it?"

"Child," she gave a haughty laugh, "how would I know?"

Enjoying another bite, Sarah asked innocently, "Didn't you make it?"

"Of course not," she answered, her nose in the air. "I have a cook."

"Oh." Sarah looked Mrs. Stately up and down. "Your dress is beautiful. I would love to make one like it."

"Child, if you come live here, you won't have to do such work. We will have it made by the dressmaker. Why, you will have a closet full of beautiful dresses."

"I will?" Sarah's eyes bugged. "Oh, I think I would like that."

"Only the finest if you become a Stately." She continued her proud look, holding her head high. "We will provide you day dresses, evening dresses, dresses to attend church, and several to wear to the balls."

Peeping at Granny, Sarah gave her a questioning look.

"A ball be kinder like a hoedown." Granny briefly rubbed her chin and then pointed at the girl. "Shore, like them barn dances back home."

"Please, Miss Evans, a ball in a ballroom is nothing like your quaint little dances in a barn full of mudsills. Ladies and gentlemen attend a ball. The first thing Sarah will need is training." Mrs. Stately's proud look had been replaced with a stern face. "She must learn how to behave properly and become a lady."

"I'm still a girl." Sarah smiled sweetly. "I have to wait until I grow up to become a lady."

The woman laughed a fake sounding, stuffy laugh. "You grow up and become a woman, but you must go to school to learn the proper ways of a lady."

"Never heared of anything like that." Granny shook her head. "Sarah already goes to school. Teached readin,' writin,' and arithmetic by the schoolmaster. She be a fine little lady now. She gonna be a school marm – a good one fer shore – good as a man." Granny winked.

"Child, you will attend the finest schools and receive the best education money can buy. You will be taught all those subjects Miss Evans mentioned, but you will learn so much more. You will be taught to walk properly, speak well, how to eat, table manners, to ride horses – oh, so many wonderful things. You *will* be a lady!"

"I all ready do those things." Sarah shrugged her shoulders. "I walk, talk, eat, use a fork and ride Blackie, Mama's horse."

"Ha!" Granny guffawed, slapping her knee. "Got ya on that one, Mrs. Stately."

In her most snooty voice, she put them down. "You both have much to learn. Whether a silk purse can be made from a sow's ear, well, that question will remain unanswered for years. I think the child can be changed – you, Miss Evans are a lost cause." Turning her face away, she stared at the roses.

Whew! The old lady chuckled to herself. *Listenin' to her, folks would think she done hung the moon.* Then, peeking at each other, Granny and Sarah kept straight faces, forcing themselves not to laugh.

In a flash Sarah's expression drooped. "I want the best education, I love to learn new things, but when will I have time for teaching school?" Her voice seemed to take on a whine. "How long does it take to become a lady?"

"Years," came the reply. "After you become a lady you will have no need for teaching. Nor will you have time."

Sarah's face grew warm and looking at Granny, she shook her head. "Mama always told me I could be a school teacher. I don't want to become a lady if I can't teach school, too. I can be a woman school teacher, and that's enough."

Her eyes became pools of water, and when she squeezed them to shut out the hurt, they ran over and down her cheeks. Jumping to her feet, she scampered into the garden.

Mrs. Stately's marble-hard yellow-green eyes, stared straight ahead. The woman never turned her head, but spoke with a hard-edged voice. "She will do things the Stately way, or she won't be coming here to live."

14

Butterfly Wings

From the woods the donkey cart slowly moved into the bright sunshine. The sun blazed hot, and the heat rippled from the fields. A sad droning song filled the air as row after row of black folks worked the crops. Tethered to a tree while his mother worked nearby, a small child played in the dirt. It made Doc's stomach churn.

The old man's shirt is wet. Reaching over Doc touched a spot about the size of a man's hand. Drawing back, he looked at his wet fingers – beet red. Fearing the worse, he smelled the crimson.

"This man is bleeding!"

"He was whipped."

"What?"

"Charlie got his-self whipped early this mornin," she went on in a matter of fact voice. "Over there's where he done got his lickin." Pointing to a three-foot post rising from the ground, she nodded, "There!"

Passing near it, Doc looked closely.

"That be the whippin' post. The overseer chains ya there, then gives the lickin.'"

"Why?" Doc's voice boomed. "What did this man do to deserve such a horrible thing?"

"He helped another slave."

"No one told us this plantation is worked by slaves. I know Christians hold slaves, but never heard of Christians beating them. Why didn't Granny's cousin tell her?" It was a question he really didn't expect the girl to answer.

114

"Massa and Mistis call it a farm."

"A farm?"

"This ain't no plantation. They says it be a farm."

The cart pulled to a stop in front of a small hut. Doc hopped out. "The Statelys are slave holders. Calling this a farm means nothing!"

Doc rolled Charlie onto his side and raised his shirt. The wounds glistened in the sunlight, and the doctor gasped. Where the whip tore the flesh the cuts oozed blood. Susie shuffled to the back of the cart. Doc's questioning eyes locked onto hers, and he tried to form the words.

Knowing his question, she answered. "He was in the big house this mornin' helpin' the cook. She was a feelin' poorly. He felts sorry for her. The overseer whipped him cause he weren't in the garden where he was suppose to work."

At the sound of hoof beats, the doctor whirled about. A black man thundering down the road and stirring dust reined his horse beside the cart. He yelled the question. "What's goin' on here, Susie?"

"It be Charlie – he done felled in the garden. You done whipped him too much. He be in a bad way."

Doc rubbed his beard. *Hmmmmm – what does she mean? Why would this black man whip another?*

The huge man dismounted his horse. Doc stood over six feet tall, but this man towered over him. With the strength of four oxen, the overseer picked Charlie from the hay as though he were a rag doll, and carried him into the hut. Then, Doc saw it – the whip. Wrapped around the saddle horn, it awaited the next slave's back.

Dear Lord, what is happening on this plantation? Shaking his head in disbelief, he entered the hut.

Waiting a moment until his eyes adjusted to the dimness, he took a quick look around. He saw one straight back chair, a small table, and the dirt floor. Charlie lay quietly on a pallet.

Immediately, Doc examined the wounds. "You did this?" He glared at the big man. Not waiting for an answer, he followed with, "Why?"

"Massa told me to. I does what I is told."

"This be the overseer," Susie explained.

"A Negro?"

The black man's face stiffened. "White man ain't gonna sit in the sun all day watchin' slaves."

While shaking his head in disbelief, Doc filled a basin from the water pitcher on the little table. He washed the old man's back.

"The overseer goes easy on the slaves when Massa ain't around." Susie's eyes brightened with a thankful look. "He's a good overseer, but Massa was up there this mornin.' Charlie had to git his lickin.'"

"Hush now, Susie. You git back to the big house. Take the white man with ya."

"I'll stay with Charlie," Doc barked. "He needs me."

The overseer walked over to Charlie's pallet. He squatted, looked the old man over, and then rose to his feet.

"You'll go now!" the black man raised his voice. "No disrespects to ya, but Massa don't want no strangers in the huts. They's for slaves only."

Doc finished washing the wounds and left Charlie lying on his stomach. His back continued to ooze red.

"I'll git a woman to look in on him later. He be up an' around tomorrow."

Slowly, Doc rose to his feet. Looking right into the overseer's eyes, he gave his diagnosis. "This man won't be up and around tomorrow – nor any other day." Whirling about, he walked from the darkness into the sunlight.

Peeking through the bushes at the edge of the woods, she saw the slave quarters ahead about a quarter mile. The overseer's place sat off by itself, at the far end of a row of huts. She had come quite a distance already. Another quarter mile was nothing for an Ohio girl used to walking miles around the farm back home.

The half-moon barely gave enough light to make out the wagon rut road, but it was enough. Always the daring one, this girl had special steel within her that other twelve-year-olds knew nothing of. There would be no turning back now. Dashing from the woods, she continually glanced left and right, keeping an eye out for trouble. Passing a small fishpond, she heard the frogs talking it up. It sounded as though they all had something to say. Finally, she neared the first hut. Squatting by what remained of a large tree, her heart thumped from excitement. For a slight moment she rested her arm atop the stump. Suddenly, feeling cold touch her arm, she tensed. Turning her head, almost afraid to look, she riveted her dark eyes on a double bit axe head, sunk deep into the wood. Another inch over and she would have sliced her arm wide open. *Whew! That was close.*

Winded from the running, she decided to sit next to the ax and catch her breath. The night remained silent, except for the singing of slaves in the distance. The girl gazed up at the black sky dotted with twinkling lights. She spotted the North Star. Watching it for what seemed like several minutes, Sarah could not help but wonder how many runaways at that very moment were using it to point their way to Canada.

Not far away, three or four coyotes broke the quiet, howling at that same moon. It sent a little chill through her. She shivered, then gathered her wits about her, and steadied herself to finish what she came for.

Hearing voices, the girl peered into the darkness. A campfire had burned down to red coals, and she scampered closer to take a peek. In a nearby branch an owl hooted its welcome as she crouched near the first hut. Suddenly the fire sparked to life when another log landed on the embers. Sarah strained to hear the words.

"It what I heard," came a voice. "White folks at the big house, and they's stayin' the night. They buyin' slaves to take them south."

"You don'ts knows that. You makin' that up."

Sarah crept closer for a better peek.

"Who that?" the first voice asked.

She stepped forward to where the flames from the campfire lit up her face. "My name is Sarah Smith. I come to see Mr. Charlie."

Jumping to his feet, the black man with the first voice, looked her full in the face. "Who with ya?" His eyes were full of fright, and they told it plain enough.

"I came alone."

"From the big house?" The disbelief could be heard in his voice. "In the dark?"

"Yes, sir. I must see Mr. Charlie, please."

"Ha," the second voice giggled. "She done called ya, sir. Git over in the light so she can see you's a slave."

"I know you're slaves. Dr. Baum told me. In the morning we're starting for home, but I can't lay my head in sleep tonight until I see Mr. Charlie."

"The white man not a slave trader?" the first voice asked.

"No, sir. He's a doctor. He and Granny brought me here to meet the Statelys. I'm an orphan and thought I could live here, but I can't. I told Granny and Doctor Baum that I would not live with people who owned slaves. Never!"

"Follow me, child," the second voice invited, her voice soft with understanding.

Leaving the light of the fire, they walked briskly along. Light streamed from one small window of Charlie's hut. Timidly, Sarah stepped into the doorway. Immediately the shadows from a single candle caught her eye as it flickered its light into the darkness. An eerie feeling gripped her body when she spotted Charlie resting on the dirt floor. Four slaves surrounded his pallet.

"This child come to see, Charlie," the second voice called from the darkness.

Everyone turned their eyes to Sarah. Moving all the way inside, she baby-stepped to the old slave's side.

"Come, angel band," Charlie moaned, his eyes closed. "Come, angel band."

Her knees buckled at the pitiful sight. Collapsing onto the pallet next to the old man, Sarah fixed her eyes on his peaceful face.

"Mama!" she whispered loudly.

The slaves peeked at each other with puzzled looks.

"Come, angel band," he gasped.

The vision of her dying mother haunted her. She had seen it and relived it time on end. Rachel's face, the buggy flying through the air, Mama's almost lifeless hand that the girl held after the accident; so many things in and out of order on that day raced through her mind.

His face, I've seen that look before. Oh, Mama, it's your face. Peaceful – so peaceful, he knows the end is near.

Tears dripped from her chin and struck the pallet. That strange coldness she endured as her mother's life slipped away, that icy cold, once more chilled her to the bone. Along with it came the same heart-wrenching fear. She took up his hand, and held on.

Once more he called out, "Come, angel band."

Looking up to his friends who gathered about the humble bed, Sarah asked, "What's he saying?"

"He's askin' for the angels to come and take him home to the Lawd," a low, soft voice answered.

"Angels?"

"Yes ma'am. The Good Book says a band of angels did come and took the soul of Laz'rit to Heaven. Ol' Charlie, he a callin' for the angels. He ready to go."

Once more she gazed into the frail face of the dying man. "I remember now – the story of Lazarus. He was the poor beggar who had crumbs to eat from a rich man's table. When he died the angels of God took his soul to Heaven. I remember!"

"Come, angel band."

"Charlie, he 'member, too. He wants to go home. Praise de Lawd for that."

"Home?"

"The slave quarters ain't his home. All his life he want the home in Glory. That be his wish."

Sarah remained by his side holding his hand. Faintly, she heard from somewhere nearby, the clear sweet voices of a people in slavery, and they filled the heavy night air with freedom songs. The evening wore on, and Charlie continued to call for the angels.

Finally, leaning close to his ear, Sarah whispered, "Mr. Charlie, you can be a butterfly and come to Ohio; we will get you to freedom. I . . .

I really wanted to tell you that, but . . . now," she choked on her tears, "I don't think you need butterfly wings. I believe your wish for a better home is about to come true."

Needing to return to her bedroom at the big house before someone realized she was gone, Sarah slowly got to her feet. Yes, she must go, but tearing herself away hit her hard. She lingered, continuing to gaze at the old man as he struggled to gain his eternal freedom.

He opened his eyes, appearing to stare, but really stared at nothing. A smile played on his lips. "Oh come, angel band," he whispered once more.

"My big wish has been to have a new home with parents, and brothers and sisters. Now it doesn't seem so important." Stooping, she gently placed a butterfly kiss on his forehead. "See you later, Charlie – in Heaven." Through eyes blurred by a rush of hot tears, she saw him for the last time. Dashing out the door, Sarah disappeared into the night.

Not long after first light, the same donkey cart crept through the horse pasture east of the house. The slaves followed close on, singing with mournful tones. The girl held Granny's hand, and watched the procession from a place nearby Charlie's flower garden.

"Sarah, ya see them Bachelor's Buttons ol' Charlie taked care of?" Granny pointed at the pretty flowers.

"Uh huh."

"I want ya to pick a few and bring them home. I cain't see Mrs. Stately a mindin' if she parts with some flowers. I'll make the fur fly if she does. Listen here, there be folks that say them Bachelor's Buttons got some kinda powers in them. Maybe they help git ya a husband. Course I don't believe such." Granny winked, giving her best shot at trying to lift the girl's spirits. "I think Charlie wants ya to have them – to remind ya of him. Press them in yer mama's Bible, give one to Mary, too."

As the funeral procession passed within fifty yards of the big house, the mood changed. Joyful praises suddenly filled the air. No longer the sad tone, the slaves sang glory songs to the Lord. Through praise songs, the slaves told everyone within earshot, they were happy Charlie had gone home to Glory.

> "Halleluiah! He has gone home,
> The Lawd welcomes Charlie at de gate.
> Praise de Lawd, Praise de Lawd,
> Praise de Lawd, for Charlie gone Home."

Sarah looked at Granny, and tears gushed from her already weepy eyes. Catching them with her hankie, she lifted her head and watched as the cart carrying Charlie's body, wrapped in a blanket, turned onto the main road. A short trip to the top of the hill, and the slaves passed from view. Rounding a bend their voices softly faded away. The field for burying slaves lay across the road, about a half-mile from the well-kept Statley cemetery.

Again Sarah dabbed her eyes and fought to keep her sobs quiet.

"Sarah, that ol' man be far better off today than he was yesterday." Granny gave her a little hug. "He got himself a right nice home, now."

"I'm sorry, Sarah," Doc added. "You've been though the mill lately, and I wish you didn't have to see this." He placed a hand on her shoulder. "Sorry we brought you here."

Sarah dropped into a chair. It was still early in the morning, but she felt tired. "I wish I knew how to feel. I'm crying because Charlie died, but I'm glad for him. That's not right, is it? Should I be happy someone died? I don't look happy, but happiness bursts in my heart. Granny, Doctor Baum, I went to see Charlie last night. I'm sorry, but I wanted to talk to him – tell him about the butterfly."

Not the time for scolding, Doc and Granny eyed each other, wondering about the butterfly remark, but remained quiet.

The doctor drew up a chair next to Sarah. Slipping a comforting arm around her, he pulled her close. "Young lady, I've been doctoring a long time, and have never told anyone, but a few times I have been glad a patient died. Good Christian folks, suffering terribly from a disease and with no hope of cure-well, they are better off going to their reward."

"Charlie is better off!" The corners of her mouth curved up a bit, and she felt her spirits begin to lift. "He'll no longer have to sleep on the dirt floor and be hit for helping someone. He didn't need the butterfly wings. He received his wish, and now he's free forever!"

Silently, the three thought about those words, free forever. They knew Charlie had to pass into the next world to realize his lifetime wish. As they stared at one another, smiles quickly broke out all around. The old slave found freedom, flown to Heaven by God's butterflies – the angels.

"Miss Mary is going to feel bad," Sarah blurted.

"What ya talkin' about?" Granny came back.

"She cried with happiness when she heard about the telegram you received asking you to bring me here. Now she'll cry with sadness."

"She'll understand," Doc assured her.

"I know." Sarah's lower lip pushed out. "Charlie had a wish, and I do, too. I want a home and parents. I don't want to stay an orphan. If I don't get parents soon, someone will want to put me on an orphan train. I won't go! I'll sneak out of the house and run away."

"Hold on there," Granny jumped in. "Now, I knowed ya had a sight more than yer share of troubles, but ya ain't goin' on no orphan train. Now that jist be a fact. I don't want ya forgittin' the Lord has a hand in yer life, too. Ya think He be allowin' the train to take ya away? No way yer a goin' west."

The old lady's words stirred Sarah's heart. She smiled shyly. "You're right, Granny!"

"Course I be right. Now lookit here, the Good Lord be a watchin' out fer ya, but He does things in His own way and in His own time. He be workin' things fer the good. Shore, I knowed ya feel like yer pushin' a wet rope up a steep hill, but think about it. The Lord provides a worm fer the robin, but He ain't a droppin' it in its mouth. Birds gotta do sompun. Mary and Doc will keep tryin' to find ya a home. So will I."

"I know God loves me. Charlie hoped for a better home his whole life. I've been an orphan just a short time. Even though I have a peck of troubles, I'll keep praying. I won't lose hope."

"A peck of troubles?" Doc gave a sideways glance.

"Shore," the girl mimicked the old lady. She loved trying to imitate others, especially Granny. Suddenly, she cracked a big smile. "Granny teached me them there words."

Doc gave another side-glance, this time at Granny. She grinned big. Then, the mood lightened as they all enjoyed a good laugh.

"Granny! I'm going to tell Mary all about our trip. She'll like hearing about Charlie – I know she will."

Jumping from her chair, Sarah pointed at the open carriage slowly making its way along the road toward the house. The driver had returned as promised.

"Let's go home," the girl squealed. "I want to see Mary, and my friend Martha, and ride Blackie, and tell the girls at church about Cincinnati, and the riverboat, and . . . and a lot of things." She paused, mainly to catch her breath. "I want to go back to school and learn, so I can become a school teacher. That's always been my first wish."

Softly, a white dove called from the garden, while another set of white and gold wings flitted from flower to flower. Sarah's eyes swiftly tracked the butterfly as it took the sweet nectar from the center of each. Then, being filled with that which keeps it alive, the beautiful winged creature fluttered away, disappearing into the blue. Scampering into the midst of the flowers, she picked a handful, and then gently buried her nose into the heavenly fragrance. After a few seconds the girl lifted her face toward the sky.

Looking bright and fresh as the flowers about her, she called out in a clear, strong voice, "Mama, ask God to give Mr. Charlie the best mansion."

Peeking over at Doc, Granny said it well. It was well spoken, indeed. "She's gonna be jist fine. Let's light a shuck fer Ohio."

What happens next in Sarah's life?

Look for the second book in the Sarah series coming soon to your favorite book dealer. *Sarah's Promise* guarantees to deliver more spine tingling excitement. Ride along with Sarah and Granny as they take the "cars" to a small hamlet in southern Ohio. Check out this passage from her next adventure:

Two rough, gawky men, entering from the rear of the car interrupted Granny's thoughts. They glowered at everyone. Smelly, with several days' growth of beard, they had not used a bathtub for weeks. Sarah's nose twitched at the odor.

Both took a seat behind Frank and Emily. The one by the window had a square head and thick neck, with a face like a used up hound dog. The other peered through greasy eyes and may have been a slight better looking. It was hard to tell since he had a crinkled up left ear, which worked against him in the looks department. Each wore a holstered gun. . . .

. . . All of a sudden his eyes narrowed to dark thin slits. "Now, here's how it's gonna be, so listen up," he thundered, terrifying the other passengers. "We ain't ridin' in this car with no blacks. You two git up and leave."

A crushing tension that seemed to crowd all fresh air from the car closed in on everyone. Sarah noticed a trickle of sweat roll down the middle of her back. Her face flushed scarlet.

"Boy," hound-face started up again, "you and yer woman can stand out on the platform, and take that brat kid with you!"

The man's voice made Sarah's skin crawl. Her heart pounded within her chest and she wanted to scream her hate for him. Yet, she knew hating him would only hurt her and he could not care less . . .

Be sure to check Sarah's website at www.sarahbooks.net
for more fun information.

e|LIVE

listen|imagine|view|experience

AUDIO BOOK DOWNLOAD INCLUDED WITH THIS BOOK!

In your hands you hold a complete digital entertainment package. Besides purchasing the paper version of this book, this book includes a free download of the audio version of this book. Simply use the code listed below when visiting our website. Once downloaded to your computer, you can listen to the book through your computer's speakers, burn it to an audio CD or save the file to your portable music device (such as Apple's popular iPod) and listen on the go!

How to get your free audio book digital download:

1. Visit www.tatepublishing.com and click on the e|LIVE logo on the home page.
2. Enter the following coupon code:
   ba4a-4188-b6cc-1e47-7c00-9f1d-c04c-2e0b
3. Download the audio book from your e|LIVE digital locker and begin enjoying your new digital entertainment package today!